Aria

By Penny Lea

Copyright © 2017 Penny Lea

All rights reserved. This book or any portion thereof may not be reproduced or used in any manner whatsoever without the express written permission of the publisher except for the use of brief quotations in a book review

ISBN: 978-1-945975-00-4

Scripture quotations are from the Holy Bible, New International Version, NIV Copyright 1973, 1978, 1984, 2011 by Biblica, Inc. Used by permission. All rights reserved worldwide.

Unless otherwise specified, hymns quoted are in the public domain.

In Chapter Two, "Twas Jesus, my Saviour, who died on the tree" is by H. Q. Wilson (1894).

In Chapter Six, the refrain "Grace, grace, God's grace…" is from "Grace Greater than Our Sin" by Julia H. Johnston (1911). "In the Sweet By and By" is by Sanford Fillmore Bennett (1868).

In Chapter Eight, the refrain "At the Cross" is by Ralph E. Hudson (1885). "Turn Your Eyes Upon Jesus" is by Helen Howarth Lemmel (1922). "Amazing Grace" is by John Newton (1779).

In Chapter Nine, the refrain "Come home, come home" is from "Softly and Tenderly Jesus Is Calling" by Will L. Thompson (1880). "Just As I

Am" is Words By Charlotte Elliott(1789-1871), and Music By William B Bradbury (1816-1868)

Published by EA Books Publishing a division of Living Parables of Central Florida, Inc. a 501c3 EABooksPublishing.com

Dedication

I dedicate this book to Brandon, who seems to have left us too soon, and to Bonnie, Roger, Christina and Aria who carry on in spite of such an untimely loss. God bless you! He will be waiting for you at the gate.

I dedicate this book to all the children who have never had a voice and to grieving mothers who have lived with pain and regret ... haunted by a tiny ghost buried deep inside. May you find the peace of the Father.

I also dedicate this book to my family who has brought much joy and delight to my life. You have encouraged me to continue on when it would have been easier to say, "I've done enough." Thank you, Harry, my dedicated husband, for sitting in your chair as you wiped tears and blew your nose until all the dogs barked uncontrollably as you read through Aria's story. Your constant comments about finishing this book worked.

I dedicate this book to the memory of dear friends who have made me a better person. To Pastor David Wilkerson who always reminded me to stay hidden in the shadow of the cross. To Sandi Weber, my dear friend, who cheers me on from heaven and still seems to remind me to "Write like you speak. Don't get into that writer's mode." How I miss you, my friend. To Bob Weber, Sandi's sweet husband, who encouraged me with text messages and many emails as I wrote late into the night. You worked so hard to get my website up and running with my music available to anyone who still wants to listen. We are praying for you, Bob, as you fight this brain tumor.

I dedicate this book to my friends who have

helped me in my ministry over all these long hard years. It's been a journey! Thank you, Tony Uriz, for helping me with all the art work for Aria and for doing art for all my Christian tracts over the span of many years. You're awesome. I know I drove you crazy, but you never complained.

I dedicate this book to the prayer warriors who intercede daily for our nation. How desperately we need the Lord! It seems hard to believe that we have strayed so far from what we were created to be. We press on, and we fight the good fight. We cry out, "Even so, come quickly, Lord Jesus." We look forward to entering those amazing gates and beholding that beautiful city. Once we see His face this will all fade away.

Introduction

In June of 2014, I had a very disturbing dream. I was standing in front of five bassinets in what seemed to be a hospital setting. As I drew closer to see the newborns, I was shocked to see their condition. They were very thin, and their coloring was gray. I couldn't tell if they were breathing. I panicked, and my heart pounded as I looked up and saw a huge angel standing behind them. He was looking straight ahead with no expression on his face.

"Do something!" I cried. "They're dying."

"You do something. You breathe life into them." His eyes were penetrating as he spoke.

"I can't. I can't!" I said in disbelief.

He stood there and said nothing. I ran to the first baby and started to blow into his tiny nose and mouth. I was shaking uncontrollably.

"Live. Live!" I shouted.

I ran back and forth from one tiny baby to another desperately trying to save them. I was shocked that the angel offered no help. One baby was not responding, and I kept going back to breathe on him.

"Leave it alone. It's dead. Move on to the rest." His words tore my heart out.

I woke up with my heart racing. I quickly sat up and put my hand on my chest trying to catch my breath.

"Dear God, What was that? Who are they?" Tears spilled from my eyes.

That morning I told my husband, Harry, about the dream, and I called my dear friend, Bob, in New Jersey. He has been working with my ministry for many years. Both were perplexed as I was, but they also assured me that God would reveal the purpose of the dream.

A couple weeks later, Harry and I were driving down the mountain in our Jeep, and I heard the word, Araha. I was so stunned that I repeated the word aloud.

"Do you know what Araha means?" I asked Harry.

"No, I've never heard that word. Are you sure you're pronouncing it right?"

"I don't know," I said, as I started typing the word into my phone. "I really don't know how to spell it, but I just heard it."

I called Bob as we weaved down the mountain past beautiful Watauga Lake. He promised he would try to help find the word and the meaning, but it wasn't easy since we weren't sure of the spelling.

A few weeks later, my Facebook friend, Bonnie, announced the birth of her grandchild. I was shocked when I saw the baby's name ... Aria.

"Harry, Look. Look at Bonnie's new granddaughter. Look at her name. That's the name God gave me. I have never heard that name in my life, but that's it!"

We stared at the picture of that beautiful baby and that unusual name. Aria. Bonnie's dad, David Wilkerson, was my spiritual father. He was such a mentor and such a blessing in my life. He had gone home to the Lord a few years before, and somehow it only made sense that he would be connected to all of this.

A few days later I sat down at my computer and started to write. From the first line, I cried. I had no idea where this story was going. I walked with the narrator through many hard and painful places, and I also walked through the beautiful gates of that glorious Kingdom and saw beauty unspeakable.

This story isn't written in the typical novel format. The scenes go back and forth from heaven to earth, so it demands concentration, but in reality, there is a thin veil between heaven and earth. Heaven is just a breath away. That's how I wrote the story. Believe me, the angels go back and forth continuously. It's not a long journey.

The story is not an easy one, but it holds much truth and beauty. Press through the difficult reads, and don't put it down. There is no condemnation intended. I wrote this with the guidance of the Holy Spirit to see lives saved. Perhaps you are one of those lives. Perhaps it's your child's life.

I realize now that the "babies" in my dream are stories that God will give to me. The Holy Spirit will birth them in me. I am the one who will breathe life into them as they are conceived in those quiet moments alone with Him and perhaps through the dreams He gives me in the night. As far as the dead child, I still have no idea about that, but He will reveal it to me in due time. I do know that many times we put much effort and time into things that will not prosper the kingdom of God. They are wood, hay, and stubble. Many times they please our own flesh, but there's no lasting effects in God's eyes.

The Lord always seems to give me the hard roads to travel. My messages are not easy ones to deliver, nor are they easy to hear. I seem to walk on a path paved with the tears of hurting people. I am a voice in a wilderness in an America who prefers a much easier path, but I know that the truth sets us free. That's my prayer for all who read Aria. I pray her story will breathe life into you.

I introduce to you the first baby in my dream … **Aria.**

CONTENTS

Chapter One—The Broken Ones

Chapter Two—The Garden

Chapter Three—Victims of Bitterness and Death

Chapter Four—Cindy's Choice

Chapter Five—Fran and Scott, a Love Story Gone Wrong

Chapter Six—Coming Home

Chapter Seven—A Timely Decision

Chapter Eight—Choices

Chapter Nine—See You at the Gate

Conclusion—It's Your Time Now

About The Author

Aria

Though my father and mother forsake me,
The LORD will receive me.

—Psalm 27:10

Chapter One—The Broken Ones

Michael

No one saw Michael walk through the crowd of protesters in front of the clinic. Though at least seven feet tall, he was invisible to all of them. He walked through the waiting room into the procedure room and saw the tiny girl lying on the table in pieces. Her mother, on another table, looked pale and worn. Tears flowed from her eyes as she stared at the stark white wall. He gently touched the young woman's arm and then turned and scooped up the pieces of her tiny child. As he did, the little one instantly became whole, and she opened her miniature eyes. She stared at his gentle face and then slowly closed her eyes. Folding her tightly under his wings, he walked out of the building, unnoticed. A single tear fell from his ebony eyes; a tear of sorrow and pain.

Michael carried her gently in his arms, holding her closely to his chest, and he smiled as her eyes glowed with wonder. The crowd had no idea that countless angels surrounded that place, but this angel had accomplished his mission. He walked past the police officers and a line of squad cars. Demons jeered and snarled at him as he passed them, but he paid no attention to such nonsense. The demons were always there.

Where there is murder, there are demons.

In an instant, he took flight with his tiny, precious cargo. His huge wings caused a gentle breeze that caressed the people below. As he and the little one neared the beautiful city, its massive gates glistened in the brilliant light.

Twelve gates were made of the most gorgeous pearl, too beautiful to describe with human words. Such a sight to behold! The walls glistened with sapphires, emeralds, topaz, and amethyst. The East gate opened, and they

entered. The streets were the purest gold …
their beauty was stunning! Music all around
seemed alive somehow, and multitudes danced
and sang, worshipping the King as He
approached the angel and the tiny new resident.

"You may hand her to me now." The
King, beautiful and regal, reached out hands
that were wounded and scarred. He was dressed
in fine linen with a belt of pure gold. His hair
was like snow, and His eyes were like flaming
torches. And that voice! It was like the sound of
many waters. As He spoke, a holy hush fell
over the magnificent city.

"She has no name." Sadness swept across
Michael's face. "She was in pieces when I went

to her. Like so many millions we have brought to you ... she was broken."

"Yes, she was broken," the King replied, "but she will never experience such pain and rejection again. It was not my plan for her to come home at this time, but they rejected her, and they robbed her of her destiny. She was to grow up and live for seventy-eight years. She was to be a musician who would touch the world with her music. She was to be a wife and a mother of three children and a grandmother of seven. She was created to represent my love through her writings and songs, but she was cut off before she was born."

"Like many millions in the garden; nameless and broken. What will her name be?"

Michael looked intently at the tiny girl. He reached out tenderly and stroked her miniature head.

"Her name is Aria." The King smiled down at the child in His arms.

"Aria … a beautiful melody. Oh! A perfect name for her. Aria!" Michael shouted.

"Yes, a lovely melody like a solo in an opera," the King whispered in her ear. "Aria has come home. You may take her to the garden. I have chosen the one to tend to her as she grows. She is part of our kingdom now. There will be no more rejection, and no more death."

The crowd sang and danced again as Michael moved on his journey toward the majestic garden west of the gate.

"Aria is home! No more pain. No more death. Home. Home to grow in His beautiful garden. Hallelujah! The child is home!" The dancing multitude sang with unrestrained joy.

Chapter Two—The Garden

In the garden, the colors of the flowers were vibrant and alive—deep purple, bright orange, stunning pink, soft and deep yellows, and reds like none on earth have ever seen. Lavender grew everywhere, and white lily of the valley grew as a border around the magnificent jeweled walls. Woven like a tapestry of His glory, it was a garden unlike anything on earth. The most beautiful flowers on the planet paled in comparison. The flowers seemed to sing with joy as they swayed back and forth; you could hear them like a gentle wind.

"He is worthy to be praised! Worthy is the Lamb who was slain, to receive power and wealth and wisdom and strength and honor and glory and praise. Worthy, worthy is the Lamb!"

The garden was filled with countless children of all ages. They all were attended to by adoring guardians. As Michael approached the garden with Aria, Brandon, a young man who appeared to be about thirty years old, stood waiting.

"I'll take her now. She has been assigned to me, and I will tend to her as she grows." He reached out his hands to her.

"She was one of the broken ones. She died a horrifying death before she was born." Michael spoke softly, looking down at the little one. Grief overtook him again, and he looked intently into the brilliant blue eyes of the young man as he handed him the child. "A treasure. A beautiful treasure rejected by those who would have been made rich by her love. I don't understand it!"

"The King grieves over these little ones, and He has cried out to His people over and over, but who has listened? They continue to be handed over to death before they have a chance to live the life He has called them to. What will become of their mothers and fathers if they don't hear the King crying out to them? What will become of their nation? What will become of their world? They will be destroyed for lack of knowledge! The spirit of murder will destroy them!"

Michael shook his head in deep concern. "Now she is yours to tend to."

Brandon could not take his eyes off the child as he stroked her face ever so gently. "Oh, they threw away such a beautiful flower! She is a masterpiece created by the Holy One. I am privileged to be chosen as her guardian. They are all masterpieces—one of a kind. Will you be coming back to the garden soon?"

Michael dropped his head. "Too soon." He turned and flew away.

"I will care for you, and you will grow like these beautiful flowers. Perhaps one day your parents will turn to the Great King, and they too will come to live here. He will offer them mercy and forgiveness, but they must receive His great gift. He is full of compassion, and His mercy knows no end. Oh, that they will hear His voice, little Aria. That is the Master's desire for all. You will understand the story of the Great King as I teach you. He has paid a great price for mankind, my little one. A great price, indeed!"

He sat down amongst the brilliant colored flowers and cradled her in his arms, and he held her close as he watched the children, a multitude of children, laughing and playing as far as one's eyes could see.

"These are the aborted ones, Aria. Like you, they were the broken ones, but look. They live. You live!"

Like a tiny seed planted in the ground, she began to spring up and grow. Brandon spoke, and she immediately understood. He taught her about the Great King, and the more he taught her, the more she blossomed and grew. The King came to the garden often. He loved to play and sing with the children. They waited for him and shouted with glee as He approached.

"The King is coming! He's coming!" they cried, as they ran to his outstretched arms.

So many new arrivals every day, yet there is always room for them. Heaven has no limits. The children are assigned a guardian who loves them with a love unknown to mankind. How does one explain love in the kingdom of God? It reaches to the highest mountain, and it flows to the deepest valley. It fills the air, and you breathe it in. It is all-encompassing.

Memories of rejection and tormenting death leave the children instantly on their arrival in this glorious kingdom. They know nothing but love, for He is love. As they grow, they learn about the Great King, and oh, how very much He loves the people of earth. The children's way of communicating would seem astounding to those on earth. It is a gift from the Father of Lights who hovers over the entire kingdom. His presence is everywhere. He gives the kingdom a magnificent, radiant light like no mortal has ever seen or dreamed of. It puts the sun to shame.

Glorious is your name, oh Lord! There is no time as we know it in this beautiful place called heaven. Learning just happens continually without any stress or effort. Wisdom is everywhere, like the air we breathe. Communication flows like a mountain stream.

In no time at all, Aria was learning and communicating with Brandon and all those around her.

"Do the people of the earth love the Great King, Brandon?" Aria asked one day as they sat together by the Great River of Life.

"Some do, Aria. His Holy Spirit dwells with them. He longs to teach them, but many turn to their own ways. They reject His love."

"But who would reject such love?" Her eyes squinted, and she looked confused.

"He came to them, but they didn't recognize who He was. They hated him because they wanted to live in darkness rather than light. They put those wounds in his hands and also the ones you saw in his feet. They killed the King of Glory by nailing him on a cross that they made from a tree. It became a tree of death. Oh, such a terrible instrument of death! They crucified the Lord of Glory."

All the beautiful trees in the garden bowed. Dew fell from their giant branches as if they were crying at the mention of this heartbreaking event, and that one of their own kind was used to crucify the Lord of Glory. They swayed back and forth as a heavenly breeze moved through the garden, and they began to sing:

"Twas Jesus, my Saviour, who died on the tree,

To open a fountain for sinners like me;

His blood is that fountain which pardon bestows,

And cleanses the foulest wherever it flows."

Aria watched the trees sadly waving and listened carefully to their beautiful song. Her light blue eyes grew huge.

"Killed? What does that mean? Died on a tree? I don't understand. Does it mean they broke Him?"

"They took his body and destroyed it. Yes, they broke Him, but He is Life. He rose from the dead! The grave could not hold Him. He gave His life for them, Aria. He allowed them to break Him, so they could live here forever in this paradise one day. They are sinful, and sin cannot enter here, so He paid the price for their sin. If they confess their sins and ask Him into their hearts, He will forgive them, and they can come here and live forever." [1]

"He loves them so much," Aria said with amazement. "All these people here in this kingdom came from earth? Did you come from there, Brandon?"

"Yes, Aria, I lived there for a time. I came here when I was thirty-two years old."

"Did I come from there, too?"

Brandon held her close. She had to learn these things, so she would become a part of the multitudes who would be interceding for the people on earth.

"Yes, Aria, you did."

"How long did I live there? I have no memory."

Brandon looked deeply into her beautiful eyes. He drew a deep breath.

"You died before you had a chance to live there. You were alive in your mother's womb. You were very much alive. Before He formed you in the womb, He knew you."

Aria looked puzzled. "I have heard that the children the King brings to this garden were broken. Was I broken like them? Was I broken like the King? Was I killed? Were all the children in this garden killed, Brandon?"

Brandon sighed. "Yes, Aria, you were broken. You were killed. Millions were killed. This is the garden of the broken ones."

"Who broke me?"

Her eyes pleaded for an answer. There is only truth in the kingdom, and this was a hard truth for Brandon to tell this little one. It was the hardest truth he would ever tell her.

"Your mother paid money for someone to break you … to kill you. She was deceived by the great deceiver. She didn't understand that you were her living daughter. They told her that you were just tissue, not a real person. She cries about her choice. It haunts her, but her heart is cold right now. She has many people praying for her. It is her choice to ask for forgiveness, and then she will find peace. She can come here and see you again if she chooses to follow the King. He died for her. He loves her."

"My mother broke me? Our mothers broke all of us? Our mothers?" Aria put her arms around Brandon's neck and squeezed him tightly.

"Aria, the holy Scriptures say this: 'Though my father and mother forsake me, the LORD will receive me.' He has received you and will continue to receive all who have been forsaken."

"I love you, Brandon," Aria whispered, wrapping her little arms around his neck. "I'm so happy you are my guardian. I know that some people here have fathers. You are like a father to me. Were you a father when you lived on earth?"

"Yes, I had a newborn daughter. I didn't want to leave her, or her beautiful mother, but the King called me here. It was my appointed time. When you come here, Aria, you would never want to go back there! We love those on earth and hope that one day they will reside here forever with all of us and the Great King. Now I am privileged to care for you, and I can watch you grow as we prepare you for the glory that lies ahead."

Brandon paused for a moment, and a look of absolute joy spread across his face. "One day we will all ride with Him when He returns to take the earth back into His hands. The evil one will no longer reign. Oh, heaven awaits that day. There will be no more killing and no more sin. May His name be forever praised! I am so thankful to be in this place. As for my family on earth … I love them, and I trust they will come here when their lives are completed. Time does not exist here like it does there. What seems to take so long on earth is just a moment in this beautiful paradise. They must get ready, Aria. They must get ready for the King!"

Aria shook her head as she took in all this knowledge. "There is much to learn." She watched some of the children playing with the puppies in the field. "What is your daughter's name, Brandon?"

A smile spread across his face. "Her name is Melody, and my beautiful wife is Kelly."

"Melody! That is like my name. My name means a beautiful melody! I love that!" she laughed. "I love that!"

"And I love that as well, my precious one. I love that so much!"

She giggled as he tickled her little tummy.

"The King named you Aria, and He put you in my care because His love is so great for all of us. His mercies are new every morning! Great is His faithfulness! I can't go to my daughter, but one day she can come to me. Her mother will raise her to love the King, but like all people on earth, she must choose to serve Him. Now, I have you to teach and nurture as you grow in this paradise. You, my beautiful, gentle song! How blessed I am."

"I'm certain that many will pray for Melody." Little Aria took his hand.

They looked at all the animals playing around their feet.

"Do those puppies have names?" She sat in the deep green, lush, velvet grass. She playfully wrapped her arms around two beautiful young dogs.

"Oh, yes," Brandon said. "This little white one is called Daisy, and that regal looking one is called Bo. Do you see that beautiful big white dog over there keeping watch near the children?"

"Yes! He is such a friend to all of us. He sits and watches us play, and it seems as though he is smiling as he watches us."

Brandon laughed, "Yes, it does appear that way. His name is Samson. He is a guardian for sure! Look over there! There is Bonita, Maggie, Buster, Casey, Max, Laura, Goldie, Teddy, Buddy, Maria, and ..."

Teddy *Little Buddy*

"Stop! You are going too fast for me to remember their names!"

She giggled with delight as he scooped her up in his arms and twirled her around. "You have an eternity to learn, my little one. We have eternity!"

A beautiful blue bird came and sat on Aria's shoulder. He sang a lovely song, and she sang along with him. It was a magical sound that no one had ever heard on earth. The music in heaven comes from multitudes and goes on continually, and yet it all comes together in one magnificent chorus. As beautiful as the music is on earth, it can't compare to the heavenly scales and the angelic notes in that amazing city.

Brandon smiled as he listened. All the animals gathered around with the children. They all sang praises to the King! Oh, yes, the animals sing. All heaven sings of the glory of God. A lamb and lion lay at Brandon's feet listening intently, and soon animals of every kind gathered around, and then they all burst into song. Oh, earth has no idea about the amazing life in heaven. Everything sings and shouts for joy!

"Aria … a gentle melody. A beautiful song," he whispered "You are a masterpiece."

Chapter Three—
Victims of Bitterness and Death

Years passed on earth and Aria's mother, Susan, graduated from medical school. She prided herself on being a successful cardiologist. She convinced herself that having the abortion while she was in her sophomore year of college was the right choice. After all, she never would have finished her education if she had been tied down to a child. At least, that's what she believed. She would have disappointed her grandparents, who were her strongest supporters since both of her parents died. When thoughts of sadness and regret swept over her, she quickly dismissed them.

Susan met Jeff five years after she graduated from medical school, and they married three years later. He was a good man who taught at the local community college. Susan never spoke about her past to him, or to anyone. It was her secret … a secret that was deeply hidden, but deadly.

Hiding something doesn't make it disappear.

They were ecstatic when they found out they were expecting a baby. Now, she could manage being a mother. Now, the timing was right, and the thought of having this baby thrilled her.

Three months into the pregnancy she miscarried. They were devastated.

Within a year, she was pregnant again. She did fine until the fifth month, and then she started to bleed. She was rushed to the hospital. The thought of losing this baby as well was more than she could bear. Friends and family members prayed for Susan and her baby daily, but she didn't believe in God. Years of education had convinced her that religion was for the weak-minded. Just a crutch.

Susan was released from the hospital and put on bed rest for the remainder of her pregnancy. The goal was to carry the baby for at least thirty-five weeks. She delivered her premature little girl at thirty-six weeks. What a beautiful baby she was! She weighed just 4 pounds 5 ounces, but she was strong and determined. Her head was topped with a reddish blonde fuzz, and her eyes were steel gray. Her tiny hands and feet were a wonder to her parents, and Susan loved counting every toe and every little finger. She and Jeff were thrilled to be the parents of this tiny, but beautiful child. They named her Jewel. A perfect choice.

Baby Jewel

"It's a miracle!" her good friend Patsy exclaimed. "So many prayers went up for you and baby Jewel."

"I had great medical care. I'm grateful for that." Susan's eyes were fixed on her newborn daughter.

"And all of us who love you are so thankful, Susan. God's hand is on you and your beautiful little girl. He loves you and your precious family."

Susan didn't respond to that, but being a mother, at last, was a joy she could hardly contain. Life was good.

Susan had developed a great reputation as a physician in her town, and she was very content with life. Jeff was climbing the ladder at the college, and little Jewel was thriving. A few years passed, and she and Jeff decided that Jewel needed a brother or sister. A few months later she was expecting, and they were thrilled with the news.

"I'm having my ultrasound in a couple of weeks, and we'll find out the gender of our baby. I can't wait!" Susan looked radiant as she shared the news with Patsy.

"I'm so happy for you and Jeff. I can't wait to hear the news. You'd better call me as soon as you know. Jewel is going to be a big sister. That's awesome!" Patsy hugged Susan's neck and finished the last of her latte.

About three weeks later, Patsy ran into Susan at the mall. Patsy had been out of town on business and hadn't talked with Susan since they had coffee together.

Aria

"Well, do you have some news for me?" Patsy rubbed her hands together with excitement.

Susan's eyes welled up, and the tears ran down her face. Patsy suddenly felt a sick feeling sweep over her as she looked at her friend and realized something was very wrong.

"I lost the baby." Susan began to cry. "I'm heartbroken. I just can't tell you how robbed and empty I feel! Now the doctors are telling me that maybe I'm just getting too old to carry a baby. That's ridiculous! I can't give up now!"

Tears spilled from her eyes as she continued. "I had an abortion when I was in college. I wasn't ready to be a mother. I lost my second child through miscarriage, and I came close to losing Jewel. Now I've lost a third child! There are three children missing from my life. Three children I never met. The first baby would be eighteen years old. I never had a chance to know any of them. They're gone. I never held them. I don't know if they were boys or girls. I don't know if they would have looked like me or Jeff ... or what they would have grown up to be!" She covered her face with her hands and sobbed.

They both stood there in the middle of the mall weeping, as people walked by staring curiously. Patsy hadn't known about Susan's abortion, or the first miscarriage.

"They're in heaven, Susan. You can see them again. As for the abortion, it's a tragedy.

So many women live with such terrible guilt and regret, but God forgives, and restores. He will restore you, and He will give you peace if you ask Him to."

"No, I did the right thing back then. I mean ... where would my life be today if I had given birth to that baby? I would probably never had finished school, or married my husband, or ..." She was silent for a moment, rubbing the tears from her face.

"No! I have no regrets at all, but I just feel so sad right now. I don't know why I told you all that. I'm just so terribly depressed and overwhelmed."

For many years, Patsy had volunteered at the local crisis pregnancy center. She knew that abortion is an unnatural act of violence to the child and to the mother. She had counseled many post abortion women, and the symptoms were not unknown to her.

Many times women live with the fact that they will never carry another child. How many times had she heard, "I killed the only baby I would ever have." So many women who have had abortions never conceive again, or they have multiple miscarriages. Many who do become pregnant have premature births, but this was certainly no time or place to have such a conversation. Susan needed healing, forgiveness, and love—and those could only come over a period of time from God the Father.

Patsy hugged Susan. "I am always available if you want to talk. I am so terribly sorry for your loss. My heart is broken for you. I promise I will pray that God will heal your broken heart, my friend. Please don't hesitate to call if you feel like talking, and please know that God is always available, Susan. He cares so much for you and your babies."

Susan had no idea that her children were in the beautiful kingdom. She had no knowledge that her first baby, Aria, was growing under the loving watch of Brandon, the angels in heaven, and the great King of Kings. She didn't realize that the son she had lost through miscarriage, and now another daughter, were safe in that beautiful kingdom as well.

How they longed to meet their mother. If only she could see that beautiful city and her precious children growing in God's garden …

But it isn't allowed. She had to seek for herself, yet she refused. She was in denial. The truth was far too painful to accept.

Chapter Four—Cindy's Choice

Cindy, a secretary at the hospital, was another sad case. She had been a beautiful girl in her early years, but following her abortion at the age of twenty-two, she withdrew from her family and friends. Her zeal for living disappeared, and her beauty was gone. Her once-beautiful red hair was now unkempt, and her skin had lost that lovely rose color. It now looked dull and gray. Her jaw was clenched, and her body was rigid. No one understood what happened to her, but she suffered from anorexia and bulimia. Now, at thirty-eight years old, she had abused her body for years. At 5 feet 6 inches and 95 pounds, she looked pitiful.

When she was able to muster up a little energy, she escorted women into the Women's Center, where she had her abortion years before. She was reaching the point of having to quit her job because of her illness. Everyone talked about her condition, and they stared at her ghastly frame. She was slowly dying, but she was in total denial. The Father of Lights had sent her many people to offer His love, but she scoffed and turned them away, rejecting the forgiveness the King offered her.

"He loves you, Cindy." Mary, a sidewalk counselor cried out to her as they stood in front of the abortion clinic one rainy Thursday afternoon.

Cindy had been escorting the women inside for several hours. The place was jammed with women coming and going.

"God sent His son to pay the price for your sins. Let Him heal you and restore you," Mary pleaded. "I know you have had an abortion, and you are deeply hurt. That's obvious, but you can see your baby again in heaven one day if only you will turn to Him!"

Cindy turned pale for a moment. How could this woman know about her abortion? She had never spoken a word of it to anyone. It was a cancerous secret that had been eating at her for years. A secret that was sucking the life out of her.

"Shut up! Jesus freak!" Cindy took the arm of a crying fifteen-year-old girl who was heading toward the front door of the clinic. She escorted her through the line of sidewalk counselors and said, "Don't listen to those liars."

"Please, let us help you," Mary cried out to the young girl. "We can help you and your baby! I beg you, don't do this!"

The poor girl looked terrified. Just a few weeks before she had her ears pierced, and her mother had to go with her to the jewelry store to sign a consent form. She couldn't even get an aspirin from the school nurse without written consent from home. Now she was making a tragic decision that would alter the course of her entire life with only strangers to reach out to her. Her parents had no knowledge and no rights. She was alone and confused. Cindy pulled her toward the clinic door as the girl looked back at Mary.

"We can help you! Please! Let us help you and your baby!" Mary cried out to no avail. They disappeared into the building.

Angels stood at attention in front of the clinic, waiting to retrieve the broken ones. Their faces showed no expression. They're always there at those places of death. Day after day, month after month, year after year they stand waiting. Waiting to retrieve little lives that are thrown away. Oh such a pity! Such a waste!

Late at night, in the darkness of her room, terror gripped Cindy. She was tormented by horrible panic attacks that left her frozen in fear. She longed for peace, but that treacherous spirit of murder that had seduced her so many years before continued to cling to her and whisper lies into her spirit. Light had gone out of her eyes long ago. Hope was gone for any peace in her life.

Her coworker at the hospital, Lisa, was a believer in the Lord Jesus, and she had been trying to reach Cindy for many years. "Cindy, God loves you, and He has a much better plan for your life than you have found. He wants to fill you with His love and His joy. He can heal you and set you free from whatever has caused you to be so hurt and angry. Please know that I'm here for you if you ever need to talk, or pray. You're wasting away, and we're all so worried about you."

"I don't need your prayers, and I'm not hurt or angry!" Cindy snapped. "I don't want your advice, or your friendship. Get out of my face!"

She got up and threw a bag of black licorice across the room. She had stuffed one piece after another in her mouth just moments before. "I hate this stuff," she muttered, as she headed to the ladies' room.

Lisa followed her. "I just want you to know that I'm here, and I would love to be your friend." She patted Cindy's shoulder and walked away.

Cindy fought back tears as she stiffened her shoulders and swiftly opened the door to the ladies' room to purge herself of the junk she had just eaten.

"Jesus freak." She hissed under her breath.

Chapter Five—Fran and Scott, A Love Story Gone Wrong

Fran and Scott were homecoming queen and king in their senior year of high school. In their yearbook they were "The Most Likely to Succeed." They met in the eighth grade, and they immediately fell in love. The two were inseparable. Where you saw Fran, you saw Scott at her side.

They had great plans for their future. They would go to college and get married after they graduated. They even talked about where they would live. They wanted a house in the country, two dogs, a cat, and three kids. It was all planned out. They both had been accepted into the universities they had dreamed of attending since junior high school.

But a problem arose. Fran became pregnant.

Scott was frantic. "You can't have it. It'll ruin our lives. We have plans for our future, and one day we'll get married and have kids, but not now. You know I love you, and we'll always be together, but we have no room for a kid in our lives right now. I'll go with you to the clinic, and it'll be all over. We can get back to our lives." His pleading ripped at her heart.

"It's our baby!" She sobbed. "We love each other, and it's a part of us. Please don't ask me to get rid of our baby!" Tears streamed down her face.

"There'll be others," he whispered, as he held her in his arms.

"But what about this one? What about this baby? You want me to kill our child? I thought you loved me."

"I do love you. If you love me you will do this for me. For us. We have a future, but this will ruin everything. Do you understand me, Fran? This will ruin our lives."

Week after week, Scott begged Fran to have the abortion, but she just couldn't do it. He made appointments, but she backed out at the last minute.

She secretly looked at baby books and learned about how babies develop. She felt an attachment to this child growing inside her body. She dreamed of what he or she would look like. She would put her hand on her belly and cry just thinking about this tiny baby that was so much a part of her love for Scott.

No one knew she was pregnant except Scott. A baby bump was starting to show, but she did all she could to hide it. She began to feel tiny fluttering like a little butterfly in her belly. Then the letter came.

Dear Fran,

You know how much I love you, and I hate to write this letter, but I must. I have pleaded with you to protect our love, but you've refused to listen. I'm not ready to be a father, and I don't believe you're ready to be a mother, but I can't reason with you. You're not listening to me, and you don't seem to care about my future, or even your own. You will always be the love of my life, but I can't be a part of this. I refuse to give up my dreams for a child I can't love. Now you're twenty weeks along in this pregnancy, and people will know. I'm so sorry, but I have to break up with you. I don't believe you love me as much as I love you, or you wouldn't have continued with this pregnancy and disrupted all our plans for the future. You've thrown them all away.

I wish things could have been different.

I love you,

Scott

"No no no … You can't. You can't leave me!" Her cries rang out, but no one was home to hear them. She ran to the phone and called him.

"Scott, you can't leave me. I thought you loved me. Please don't leave me. I will do anything. Anything to hold on to what we have!" She sobbed into the phone. Her body shook.

His voice broke. "I love you too, but it has to be this way. I can't do this, Fran. I can't. There's just too much at stake. I did find a place in Jersey that can still take care of this. It's a longer procedure, but it's safe. It's called a partial birth abortion. They do them on late-term women all the time, so they can still help us. I can make the appointment, but you have to go this time. No more backing out, or we break up."

"Okay. Okay, Scott. I'll go. I promise. I can't lose you." She sobbed into the phone as she put her hand on her protruding belly.

"I'll call right now." He hung up the phone.

She ran to the bathroom and threw up.

***

A little over a week later, on a July afternoon, they walked into the clinic. Fran held on to Scott's arm with every ounce of strength she had.

"It's fine, babe. You'll be fine. It'll all be over soon, and we can get back to our lives."

Tears streamed down Fran's face as they called her name. She gave Scott a pleading look as she headed for the door, but he just nodded at her and whisked his hand, telling her to go.

She lay on that cold table and clenched her fists. The abortionist walked in. He was cold and impersonal. He said nothing to her.

The attending nurse never made eye contact. "It may be a bit uncomfortable because he has to turn the fetus if it isn't in a breech position. You may be lucky, and it may be turned with its feet down."

The words seemed like a bad dream. She was somewhat drugged from the pill they had given her, but she was very much aware of what was happening. Excruciating pain ripped through her body as the abortionist pulled the baby out feet first. She thought she felt little feet moving.

The rest of the child's body was pulled out, but his head was still inside her body. The nurse watched the baby's hands clasping and unclasping. She saw his tiny feet kicking. She showed no emotion.

A nightmare! The abortionist picked up scissors and stabbed the little boy at the base of his skull. His tiny arms jerked out in a flinch, a startled reaction, like a baby does when he thinks he might fall. The scissors were spread open to enlarge the opening. The abortionist then took a high-powered suction catheter and inserted it in the opening and turned it on. It sucked the baby's brains into a jar. His skull collapsed, and he went limp. The nurse took the tiny body and set it on a table.

Fran turned to see what she was doing. "Is that my baby?" shock overtook her.

"Yes," the nurse said.

"Is it a boy or a girl?" Fran was so weak she could barely get the words out. The room spun. Her body shook from head to toe. Nausea swept over her.

"A boy," the nurse mumbled coldly. She quickly turned away.

No one saw Michael enter the room, but he stood there next to Fran. He had arrived immediately after the baby died. As with Aria, he gathered the little boy in his arms and tucked him under his wings. Pain etched his face as he looked back at poor Fran. She was hysterical.

He walked out of the procedure room, through the crowded lobby, and passed through the crowds on the street. He took flight and headed for the gates of the Great City with another tiny, broken child. The little boy's earthly remains were strewn on a blue pad on the cold metal table like garbage.

It was some time before Fran had the strength to walk. Scott waited nervously for her. He smiled when the nurse escorted her weak body into the waiting room, but he fought hard to cover his shock when he saw her condition. He stood up and he put his arm around her. "It's all over now, babe."

The nurse was cold and impersonal. "If she has any complications, take her to the emergency room. Do not bring her back here."

"Complications?" Scott tried to hide the look of concern.

The nurse shoved a page listing several possible complications at him. "As I said, if she has any problems take her to a hospital. We will not see her here."

She turned around and quickly walked away.

Scott held Fran's arm tightly as they slowly walked outside. She was so weak she could barely make it to the car. Heartbreaking! A pitiful sight.

"It was a boy." Her voice trembled as tears rolled down her face. "It was a baby boy. He was alive when they pulled him out, but they killed him. We killed him! We killed our son, Scott. Oh, my God! We killed our little son. My baby. Oh, God. My baby!" She put her hands on her belly and burst into uncontrollable sobs. Scott sat there stunned. Oh, so dreadful.

She sat in the front seat, dazed. Scott said it was over, but it wasn't over.

The nightmare had just begun.

Would she wake up and discover this was a terrible dream? No, but she would wake up night after night tormented for years as the pictures of her broken baby flashed through her mind, a living nightmare. It would put her on a dreadful course that she had never dreamed she would encounter. It would rob her of her plans for her future, and it would imprison her in guilt and regret.

Scott left for college a few weeks later. He told Fran he would call as soon as he was settled, but he never called. In spite of her constant phone calls, he was out of the picture and out of her life. She never heard from him again. The love of her life was gone, and her baby was dead.

She cancelled her plans for college. She was suicidal. She took several pills one night, but she didn't die. It wasn't her time. The ambulance raced her to the hospital, and they pumped her stomach.

She didn't see the angel who stood beside her as she lay in the hospital bed, but he was there. Oh yes, he was there.

A nurse came in that night. "I just want you to know that God loves you. He has a plan for your life. He forgives you for all your wrong choices, and He desires to take you home to His kingdom one day when it is the right time."

She handed Fran a little wordless booklet that shared the love of Jesus with colorful pages. "The colors tell the story. It's a beautiful love story. If I can ever help you, please call me. I put my phone number on the little book." The nurse patted Fran's hand. "Close your eyes and rest."

Fran turned away and threw the little book across the room "There is no God!" She buried her face in the pillow and cried.

The day Fran was released from the hospital she packed her things in her overnight bag. She saw the little booklet lying on the night stand. She had tossed it away, so what was it doing there? She threw it in her bag and walked out.

A few months later she was sitting alone in a bar. She drank a lot now, and she had no friends left. No one understood why she had pulled away. Her parents were totally confused and heartbroken because she had distanced herself from them as well. They had always been so close, but now they rarely heard from her. A few women sitting near her at the bar struck up a conversation. They were blasting men in general, and Fran jumped in on those remarks.

"I hate men. They're all users." Her words were like venom as she spewed them out.

"I totally agree." The brunette sipped her gin and tonic and put her arm around Fran's shoulder. "Who needs them?"

Their words were slurred after several drinks, but the bashing continued. One comment topped the one before. It went on for two hours.

"Let's stay in touch. We get together often. There's a group of us, and I think you would be a welcome addition." The short blonde flashed a smile as she handed Fran her phone number. She and her friends stood to leave.

In a matter of months, Fran was a big part of their group. Her new friends fueled her anger. She thought she had found her place, but she didn't realize that you can run, but you can't hide from the living God. She would learn that lesson much later.

The nightmares and the flashbacks continued to haunt her. She lived every day with the knowledge that she had killed her little boy. She played the scene over and over in her head. She was locked inside a horror too terrible to share with anyone.

She hated herself, and, oh, how she hated Scott.

The world is full of broken people. They hurt, and they're filled with rage. They're rejected, and they're eaten up with pain. They try to hide from the all-knowing eyes of a loving God who longs to take them under His wings and comfort them. God, the Father of Lights, sent His son into the world not to condemn the world, but that through Him they might be saved. [2]

Like a lamb, He was led to slaughter, yet He said nothing. He paid the price that we should have paid. For our sins He was wounded, and for our evildoings He was crushed, He took punishment by which we have peace, and by His wounds we are made well. [3]

Poor Fran. The truth was in that little book the nurse had given her … the little book that she never looked at. It was shoved in her dresser drawer with all kinds of junk.

Every July she was haunted by the little ghost of her son lying on a blue pad on a cold table in that abortion clinic. The picture never left her mind. It played over and over. She watched mothers with their babies and felt robbed. Sometimes she sat quietly and put her hand on her belly, trying to remember the tiny fluttering.

Every day that passed brought new questions and more tormenting thoughts. *He would be two years old now*, or *He would be five years old now*.

Many times she sat near the park and watched children playing on the playground. Thoughts constantly ran through her mind, and she'd ask herself questions like, *I wonder if he would like baseball. He would love that merry-go-round and those swings.*

Would he like the merry-go-round and the swings?

As she stared at the children she would think, *He would be about that tall by now.*

Would he have dark hair like that little boy?
Would he like music? Would he look like me?
What color were his eyes?

Torment.

Scott finished school and landed a good job as a civil engineer. He married and had three children of his own. The experience of being a dad brought forth the guilt and shame of what he had done so many years before. He never spoke of it, but it haunted him as he looked into the eyes of his children. There was one missing … a son. Fran's words rang in his ears.

It was a boy. They killed him. We killed him! We killed our son, Scott. Oh, my God! We killed our son.

One night he sat alone in his living room holding the remote and flipping through channels. He saw a man on TV preaching to a huge crowd. He tried to change the channel, but the remote didn't work. He pressed it again and again, but it seemed to be frozen.

"You have made choices that you regret. You're in pain deep inside, and you feel trapped. You have nowhere to turn. God knows your pain! He has seen all your sins, yet He sent His son, Jesus Christ, to die on the cross in your place. You can't fix it, but He can. I am asking you to get out of your seats and come to Him. Let Him save you. Trust Him, and ask Him to come into your life tonight. This is the day of your salvation! If you are watching at home, bow your head and pray that Jesus will come to you and forgive you. He will. Go ahead. Call out to Him right now. Receive Him as Lord and Savior tonight."

The words stung Scott like a sword plunged into his heart. He cried like a child.

"I killed my son." He sobbed. "I made her do it. I made Fran do it. I destroyed her as well!" He fell to his knees on the living room floor. "Forgive me. Please forgive me. Come into my heart. I receive you tonight. I choose you as my Lord and Savior. I'm so sorry. I'm so sorry!"

His sobs were cries of repentance. An angel stood next to him, and then another, and another. Soon the room was full of angels, and

God's glory saturated that place. The angels sang and rejoiced!

Demons who had held Scott captive for so many years stood far off in the corner. They cowered at the sound of his prayers and the singing of the angels. The spirit of murder had to flee because the presence of the Lord filled the room. The demons shrieked and disappeared through the walls.

"Another child has come home. Worthy is the Lamb who was slain. Worthy! Worthy! He whom the Son sets free is free indeed.[4] Scott is free. He is no longer in chains." The angels shouted, danced and rejoiced as they always do when one sinner comes home.

Yes, every life is a treasure.

That night belonged only to Scott, but soon Scott's wife, Tara, and their children would learn of this great salvation, and they too would come into the truth of God's love. Oh, how glorious! Scott didn't yet know that wonderful promise, "Believe in the Lord Jesus Christ, and you will be saved, and your household."[5]

Chapter Six—Coming Home

Aria sat with Brandon in the garden. The aroma of the lilies of the valley, the rose of Sharon, the magnolias, the lilacs, and all the hundreds of other flowers was exhilarating. The whole kingdom was filled with this glorious fragrance. They talked of many things, and they had deep discussions about those on earth. They so hoped that Aria's mother, Susan, would hear God calling her, but there was a question Aria had to ask Brandon.

"What about my father? We never speak of him. Did he know that I existed?"

"Your mother never told him about you, Aria. He has no knowledge of you. He was young, and he made mistakes, but as he's grown older his heart has become more sensitive to the voice of the King. He's on a good path, and he's seeking truth, but the enemy constantly tries to distract him. People are praying for him. We must believe that he will hear the voice of the Great Shepherd soon. His time on earth is running short."

"What is my father's name?" Aria's eyes sparkled as she looked up at Brandon.

"His name is Joel." Brandon put his arm around Aria and drew her tightly to himself.

"Joel and Susan ... my father and mother." A look of love radiated from Aria's beautiful face.

Aria and Brandon held hands and sang a beautiful song of love and deliverance for the young man who had never met his daughter.

Joel was forty-two years old, and he had no idea that he had exactly 272 days, 17 hours, 22 minutes, and 3 seconds left on the planet.

He occasionally attended church, but the enemy did all he could to block out the voice of the King. Steve, his one Christian friend, witnessed the love of Jesus to Joel on many occasions.

"If today you hear His voice, harden not your heart."[6] Brandon spoke the scripture aloud. "May he hear the voice of the Great Shepherd and be moved by the mighty wind of the Holy Spirit. Oh, that Steve's words would penetrate his heart. Great Father of Lights, pursue and capture Joel's soul!"

"When will it ever end, Brandon? They just keep coming!" Aria watched as another broken child was brought into the garden. She was maturing and gaining such heavenly wisdom. Her songs filled the garden. She was a gentle soothing melody of God's love to all who came there. Everyone loved her songs. She began to sing.

"Jesus loves the children. He gave life to them!

Bride of Christ, Rise up I pray!

Don't let them die before their time. He has a plan for each young life!

Bride of Christ, Rise up, I pray!

Turn to Him, and choose His ways. He's

calling out to you.

You can save them if you will!

Bride of Christ, Rise up, I pray."

Her songs of intercession and praise filled the garden. Her melodies were like a holy offering going up as incense to the altar of heaven.

"Their hearts have become cold." Brandon stroked Aria's hair. "They face a terrible judgment if they continue to sacrifice their children to their gods of choice. Soon the King will return to earth as King of Kings and Lord of Lords! He came first to earth as the lamb, and He sacrificed His life for all of sin, but He will come back to earth as a lion.[7] He will come across the sky like lightning from the East to the West.[8] He will have fire in His eyes and a sword in His hand. He will ride on the back of that beautiful white stallion."

He looked down at Aria and picked her up in his arms. "Multitudes of us from heaven will ride with Him. He will avenge the blood of the innocent on that day. It will be a great and a terrible day! Many will cry out for the rocks to fall on them because they will be terrified to look at the one they have rejected."[9]

"When will we ride? Aria asked, with a tone of excitement in her voice.

"No one here knows for sure, but we do know that it will be soon. The Church on earth senses it. They know He is coming, yet, sadly, many still slumber."

***

One day as Aria and Brandon were passing by the beautiful pearl gates, they saw a young woman being escorted through the gate by a glorious angel. A little girl holding a brilliant bouquet of flowers stood waiting as the woman entered.

"Mother!" she cried.

The woman held on to the angel's arm with a look of amazement. She gasped. "Who is that lovely child?"

"She's your daughter. Her name is Grace. Don't you remember, Sharon? You named her many years ago." The angel smiled at the child.

Sharon had become pregnant when she was eighteen years old. Her father was the pastor of a large church, and the thought of disgracing him horrified her. Ben, the young father of the baby, came from a prominent family in the church as well. The couple just couldn't deal with the embarrassment it would bring to so many if they had their baby, so they made an appointment for the abortion.

When their parents finally found out about the child, they were devastated. They ministered to Sharon and Ben, but it would take years before any of them could get over the fact that the baby had been killed in such a horrible way.

"I pastor a large church, but I have lost a grandchild to this monster of abortion, and my daughter is deeply wounded." Sharon's dad broke down and wept. "What have I done wrong that she felt she couldn't come to me? It seems that I can help everyone else, but I failed my own daughter!"

"We both failed." His wife's hands trembled as she wiped her tears.

Everyone was filled with guilt. The pastor and his wife, Ben's parents, and all the family members. Many in the congregation felt they had let this young couple down as well. Friends who had kept Sharon and Ben's secret were plagued with regret for not speaking up, and then there were those who drove Sharon to the abortion clinic. They all felt responsible for the death of the little child and for the deep wounds in the hearts of this young couple. They all needed God's grace and healing to survive.

They all needed forgiveness.

Oh, the lives that are ruined when the spirit of murder creeps into the soul and devours truth and love. He is the father of lies! Beware!

Sharon found forgiveness with the help of family and friends. Ben also came to Jesus. Years after her abortion, she realized that her baby deserved a name. She named her Grace.

Now, Sharon stood inside the gates of heaven looking at a little girl with glimmering blonde hair that sparkled like diamonds. The child stood there holding the bouquet of deeply colored flowers of yellows and purples. Many of Sharon's family and friends were waiting as well. They were there to welcome her home.

"I asked God's forgiveness for taking her life, and I named her at that healing meeting at church, but I never dreamed she would meet me at the gate! I never dreamed she could love me after what I did!" Sharon's eyes were glued to Grace.

"You were forgiven, Sharon." Jesus embraced her. "There is no unforgiveness in this kingdom. My grace is sufficient."

The Lord smiled at her and nodded his head at Grace. She ran to her mother, handed her the flowers, and threw her arms around her waist. "Mother, I have been waiting for you. Welcome. Welcome home!"

What a beautiful sight! There was such joy in heaven over that reunion. Singing broke out all over the kingdom as the two of them walked together for the first time.

The angels shouted praises. "May God be forever praised. Worthy is the Lamb! Worthy is the Great Redeemer. He has set the captives free. Free at last. Free at last!"

The multitudes sang,

"Grace, grace, God's grace,

grace that will pardon and cleanse within;

grace, grace, God's grace,

grace that is greater than all our sin."

The animals sang. The flowers and the trees sang. Everything is so full of life in heaven, and all heaven sings. Oh, such worship. No one on earth has ever experienced such worship. Praise to the Lord on high. Great is the Lord and greatly to be praised!

It's a beautiful thing to see God's people come home to the kingdom. It's where we belong. Earth is not our home. We're there for a very short time, and while we're there it's so important to find our purpose. Our time on earth is a preparation for eternity with the one who created us, so we must be careful not to waste that time on trivial things that will have no value later. Our life on earth is but a vapor, but heaven is eternal joy. Each one who enters through those beautiful gates comes into the

city with looks of wonder and awe.

***

Sandi was one dear soul who had waited

with great anticipation for her homecoming

celebration. She was ecstatic as she entered the

great city. She had suffered with diabetes since

her early childhood, and it had taken a terrible

toll on her body over the years. She had come to

Jesus in her twenties, after falling deep into the

ditch of sin and disgrace. She was exuberant

when she met the Lord, and she became a

mighty witness to many as she shared her story

of deliverance and grace. Her testimony

changed so many lives!

When she and Robert married, it was like a dream come true for both of them. They longed to have children, but she became pregnant twice and miscarried both babies. They were devastated. They were blessed to adopt two beautiful girls a few years later, and they loved those children with all their hearts.

God is so good! He dries our tears, and He heals our broken hearts. He fills the void that no man can fill.

Sandi often talked to her friend, Leah, about her babies in heaven. "I know they're waiting for me. I know that the Holy Spirit has revealed to me that I have a son and a daughter there in that beautiful garden. The thought of meeting them in heaven is one of my greatest joys. I can't wait to see them!"

Leah had also miscarried two babies. She had five children after those miscarriages, and when people asked her how many children she had she would say, "I have five children here and two children in heaven."

She and Sandi were best friends, and they were a great encouragement to each other. A friend is a wonderful blessing, a treasure that should never be taken for granted. A true friend loves at all times. Such a gift!

Sandi lived to be sixty-four years old. Toward the end of her life, she was very fragile and worn out. She was confined to a wheelchair for several years, and her body just couldn't fight off all the infections as she aged. No one wanted her to leave, but she knew that God was calling her home.

"It's time." Her words pierced Robert's heart as they sat in the hospital room. "He is calling me home. You must let me go."

"I can't let you go. Please. You can fight this. We can fight this together. What will I do without you? You're my best friend. I don't want to go on without you!" Tears streamed down Robert's face.

"God loves you, and He will take care of you and our girls. You know that I love you, Robert. You are the love of my life, but Jesus is calling me home. I'm very tired, and I must go."

She left the world behind on Mother's Day. It was a terribly sad goodbye, as it always is for those of us who are left behind, but hold on. Oh, the joy that lies ahead! There is a great reunion ahead for those who love Jesus.

There's a land that is fairer than day,

And by faith we can see it afar;

for the Father waits over the way

to prepare us a dwelling place there.

In the sweet by and by,

we shall meet on that beautiful shore;

in the sweet by and by,

we will meet on that beautiful shore.

Now Sandi was at the gate. She was young again! Her beautiful long dark hair fell down her back, and her emerald green eyes glowed with wonderment. She, like all the rest, was greeted by a host of saints and angels.

Jesus stood to the left of the gate and watched. Two children approached her with flowers. A beautiful little girl with flowing dark hair who appeared to be about eight years old held the hand of her brother, who looked to be about four years old. His hair was light blonde, and his eyes were the color of the sky. She gasped with joy as they walked toward her.

They held out their bouquets to her, and the little girl said, "Welcome home, Mommy. We are Ivy and Nicholas. We're so happy to see you. We knew you would come. We've been waiting. So many have been waiting for you! Will daddy be coming soon?"

"Oh, yes." Her eyes danced with delight. "He will be coming very soon, and your sisters will be coming as well."

Sandi stood in total amazement. She had longed for this day for so many years, and now she was standing there looking at the children that she had lost in her early weeks of pregnancy so many years ago. These were her children from the moment of conception. They were beautiful spirits who came from a loving God, and now they were standing there together in the City of the Great King. Yes, before He formed them in the womb, He knew them![10]

Oh, the look of wonder and joy on all of their faces! They ran to her, and she whisked them up in her arms. Singing filled the kingdom as the three of them joined hands and sang and laughed and danced. Oh, how they danced. It was a circle of love that could never be broken. Never!

Jesus put His arms around them. "Welcome home, Sandi, daughter of mercy and grace." A smile spread across His radiant face. The Prince of Peace bowed and extended His hand. "Dance with me." Such a dance! A dance one could only dream of. "Eye has not seen, nor ear heard, nor have entered into the heart of man the things God has prepared for those who love Him."[11]

What a celebration! No more memories of loss, pain, sin, and sickness. All of that had been left behind on planet earth. Now there was endless celebration and joy. This is heaven.

This is eternity.

Chapter Seven—A Timely Decision

Steve and Joel were having a deep conversation at Steve's apartment on the night of September 27. They were both musicians, and they spent most of their time working their day jobs and playing music on weekends, so personal time was limited.

"You need to make a decision, Joel." Steve put his hand on Joel's shoulder. "We're getting older, and we have no idea what each day will bring. You're my friend, and I want to see you in heaven one day. What are you waiting for?"

"I don't know, Steve. I believe that Jesus died for me, but something keeps holding me back. I know that I need Him in my life, but …"

"Why not make a decision right here and now, Joel?" Steve prompted. "I will pray with you, and you can ask Him into your heart. I feel strongly that you need to settle this once and forever. We're not promised tomorrow."

Angels stood around the men, but demons also gathered and clung to the walls. Heckling and mocking, they tried to steal Joel's attention. They're masters of deception and confusion. They're hideous, impish, dark, disgusting creatures. They come from the father of lies.

"Liar! Liar!" they yelled. "Don't listen to that lunatic. Not today. No. Not today. Go home now. Go home, Joel!"

One of the angels pulled a golden sword from the sheath on his waist, and the demons immediately hushed and cowered.

The men could not see any of this, but Joel felt distracted by something, yet his heart was being pulled toward the Truth.

"I want to do that, Steve. I want to accept Jesus." Tears spilled over and ran down his face.

One of the demons screamed, "Nooo. Nooo! Not now, you fool. You fool. Not now!"

The angels drew closer and surrounded the men.

"Just talk to him, and He will hear. You don't need any fancy words." Steve put his hand on Joel's shoulder again. They bowed their heads, and Joel began to pray.

"Lord, I have made a lot of mistakes. I don't know what has held me back for so long, but I don't want to be held back any longer. Please forgive me of all my many sins, and come into my life. Make me the person you created me to be. I lay my life at your feet. Thank you for dying in my place. May you be glorified in me. I receive you now as my Lord and Savior. In Jesus' name, amen."

The angels rejoiced and sang as the demons fled the room whining, spitting, and cursing. Steve put his arms around his good friend, and they both wiped tears that couldn't be restrained.

"You're part of the family of God now, Joel. Nothing can snatch you out of His hand. Nothing. Not life, not death, nor principalities, or powers. Nothing can separate you from the love of God."[12]

They talked for a long time, and they read many scriptures together. Steve pulled a Bible out of his drawer and gave it to Joel before he left.

"I bought this for you a while back. I've been waiting for this night for a long time, Joel."

Joel opened the Bible and wrote, *September 27, 2014. The day I was born into the Kingdom of God.*

"Never forget this date, Joel. You are reborn in Him. He lives in you now. This is food for your soul. The more you read it, the more you will grow. This is His Word to you."

It was 4 a.m. when they looked at the clock.

"Time flies when you spend time with Jesus!" Steve was shocked at where the time had gone.

"Man, I've got to get home and get some shut-eye before work. At least I don't go in until noon." Joel pulled his keys from his black leather jacket.

Joel left the apartment feeling alive and light. The heaviness was now gone. He devoured that Bible. He took it to work, and he read it on break. Any time he could find a few minutes during the day he pulled away and read. He got up early and had his devotion time, and he spent time every night studying. He talked with Steve daily, and they got together every chance they could to study.

"I feel like a new person."

Joel's words thrilled Steve. "You are a new person in Christ Jesus. Old things have passed away, and all things have become new."[13]

Steve not only had a good friend in Joel; he had a new brother in Christ. It was awesome!

On October 22, 2014, Joel was headed home from work. He and Steve had planned a cookout and a Bible study for that evening. Joel had his guitar in the back seat, and he was excited to share the beautiful new song he had written about Jesus with his friend.

"It's the first of many worship songs to you," he whispered to the Lord.

He was two blocks from home.

A black Suburban raced through the red light. The sound of crashing metal. A fiery explosion. Joel never knew what hit him.

He was pinned inside his burning blue Subaru, but the impact had killed him immediately. It was 5:22 p.m. when Joel left the planet to go home to Jesus.

Blue lights flashed and sirens screamed as the angel escorted Joel from the wreckage. Joel and the angel walked right through the crushed metal and scorching flames. Joel looked back and saw the firemen fighting the blaze. Paramedics raced frantically toward the mangled vehicle.

"We need more help! Get more help," the firemen yelled, hoping there was some way to pull the young man from the burning heap of metal.

Shattered glass was everywhere, imbedded in Joel's face, his body, and his black leather jacket. The front seat was stained with blood, which dripped onto the Bible that lay on the floorboard. The guitar was shattered and jammed against the back seat.

A terrible sight, but that body no longer belonged to Joel. His eyes turned back to the angel who held him by the hand.

"It's time to go, Joel."

In a twinkling of an eye, they entered the beautiful gate.

Brandon took Aria by the hand. "Let's take a walk to the East gate. There's someone I want you to meet."

Joel entered the city with a look of joy and astonishment on his face. His grandfather, whom he had loved so dearly, was the first to greet him. Many relatives and friends cheered as he entered the kingdom. Angels celebrated.

King Jesus stood next to Brandon and Aria. They all smiled with delight. Aria had picked some lilies of the valley on their way and held them lovingly as she watched.

"Is it him? Is that Joel, my father?" Aria jumped up and down. Her beautiful blue eyes sparkled with excitement.

"Yes, Aria." The King scooped her up in His arms. "He is home now. You must go and greet him."

Aria ran to Brandon and hugged him tightly. Taking his hand, they made their way through the cheering crowd. Aria stood there in front of Joel and held the beautiful bouquet of delicate white flowers out to him.

"How beautiful you are!" He stooped down to take the flowers. "What is your name?"

"My name is Aria." She handed him the bouquet. "I've been waiting for you. Many here have been waiting for you. We have longed to see you. She wrapped her arms around his waist.

"I rejoice in that! Have we met before on earth? I don't know how I could ever forget such a beautiful face. Were all these people waiting for me? I know many prayed for me for years. I want to thank them."

"I did. I prayed for you." Brandon glowed, as he walked toward Joel.

"Brandon. Brandon!" Joel cried out. "My brother. My brother!" They embraced and laughed as Aria stood amazed.

"Joel is your brother? Joel is your *brother*?" she marveled.

"Who is this little girl with you?" Joel kneeled down and put his arms around Aria.

"She's your daughter." Brandon embraced the two of them.

"But I don't have a daughter." Joel looked up at Brandon with a priceless look of surprise.

"Oh yes, Joel, indeed, you do have a daughter. You never met Aria. She came here before she was born. I've been her guardian. I've been privileged to care for her since she arrived."

"Before she was born?" Joel looked at this beautiful child with a look of wonder. He gently pulled her up into his arms. Love for her consumed him.

"Yes. Before she was born." Brandon looked down at Aria.

He squeezed her hand as he continued. "There is much prayer going up to the throne for her mother, Susan. We can only believe that the people of God will continually pray for all the mothers and fathers on earth. Millions of children have been sacrificed on the altars of convenience and choice. Young parents have been wounded and destroyed as well. Prayer is a powerful force in this terrible war on children.

They must pray more. The Church on earth must pray!"

"I never knew. I never knew about you, Aria. Oh, My precious Aria. How beautiful you are." Joel held her close and kissed her lovely cheeks over and over. He had never known such joy! This was heaven. Heaven! A place of joy unspeakable and full of glory.

He looked up and saw King Jesus standing in front of them. His eyes were like pools of living water. Gentleness and love poured from them. A magnificent crown had been placed on Joel's head on his arrival. Joel knelt before the King, laid the beautiful crown at the feet of Jesus and worshipped him. All of heaven bowed and worshipped the King.

"Welcome home, my son." Jesus took Joel's hands in His. He lifted him up and embraced him. "Welcome home!"

The angels broke out in song. *"How great is our God. He is worthy of all praise. His greatness no one can fathom!"*

All of heaven rejoiced at such a beautiful reunion!

"Worthy is the Lamb to receive glory and honor and power. He is the great One. The Holy One. Worthy. Worthy is the Lamb. He is the Father to the fatherless. He is the Great Shepherd. He is the bright and Morning Star!"

A multitude of saints united their voices in song. Oh, such a symphony of love and praise. A heavenly opera of worship!

Chapter Eight—Choices

Years passed on earth, and Cindy was now eighty-four pounds. Although so many people had reached out to her, she rejected the Lord and any help from those who loved her. Cindy was lying in a hospital room in Texas, and her aging parents sat at her bedside, speechless and hopeless. She was passing away. They couldn't understand what had happened to their once-vibrant daughter. She had always loved life and was filled with such joy as a child, and then one day she just changed abruptly.

They had no idea about the baby that she had aborted. Now, as she was close to drawing her last breath, they were numb after years of suffering. They suffered as much as she did as they helplessly watched their daughter fade away. They too were victims of her choice, but they didn't realize that terrible truth. Yes, abortion has many victims. A child dies, and so many others suffer. The tentacles of this deadly spirit of murder spread out and strangle the joy of life out of so many. Such a tragedy!

Reverend Martin, the hospital chaplain, came into the room and walked up to Cindy's bed. "May I pray with you, Cindy? Have you ever asked Jesus to forgive you of your sins and to be your Lord and Savior? He paid the price for your sins and mine. It's not His will that any should perish, but that all would have eternal life. Will you ask Him into your heart? I will help you pray."

Cindy turned her head away. "No." Her weakened voice drifted. "I don't need Him. Go away."

Her parents wept as they held tightly to one another.

"I'm so sorry." Pastor Martin gave them a look of pity, and he sadly walked out.

The room suddenly seemed very cold. Cindy's mother felt a piercing chill pass by her body. Cindy suddenly sat up and her eyes widened with a look of terror. She seemed to be looking at something at the bottom of her bed. She screamed. "No!" Her mouth dropped open as she gasped one time. She fell back and died.

Impish dark creatures celebrated as they surrounded her body. "We won. We won. She's ours!" They screeched in celebration as they pulled her spirit from the room. There were no angels this time … only darkness and despair.

We choose darkness, or we choose light. The enemy dwells in darkness, and those who reject the King of Kings make a treacherous choice. It's never God's will to see anyone die like Cindy. He longs for us to come to the light of His love. Why would anyone reject such a gift?

Houses on earth, even the most beautiful, could never compare to those in the Kingdom. Heavenly mansions line the streets in brilliant colors. Staircases of gold, floors embedded with jewels and mother of pearl, and exquisite tapestries such as no king on earth has ever possessed will be ours. This is joy unspeakable! Heaven is a place of wondrous activity and endless praise and worship to the Great Shepherd and the Father of Lights. This is our reward when we choose Him.

Children play, laugh, and sing constantly. The great River of Life flows through the city, ducks swim in aqua-colored ponds, and animals graze with joyous freedom. The mountains tower gloriously around the entire kingdom, and the emerald rainbow that circles the throne of God is a continual promise of eternity to those who reside in this glorious place.

The children, along with all the residents in the kingdom, sing songs of intercession for the people on earth. They long for them to find the Truth and the Light. They know that there is a veil between heaven and earth. It's up to the King if the veil is ever drawn back for a time. Occasionally that does happen. There are small glimpses on both sides. That veil was pulled back ever so slightly for Jared, one of the broken ones.

One night, as Scott was sound asleep, he had an amazing dream. He saw a young curly-headed blonde boy standing before him. The child was holding a little flower out in front of him. He smiled at Scott and then disappeared.

Scott sat up abruptly and reached out to the child, but he was gone.

"That's my son!" he shouted aloud. "That's my son!"

Tara, Scott's wife, shot straight up in bed. "Scott, what's the matter? You must have had a nightmare."

"No, I didn't have a nightmare, Tara. I saw my son. I saw my son!" Tears flowed. "I have to find Fran and tell her that I'm sorry. I saw our son in a dream, and I want her to see him one day in heaven. I've heard stories about Fran from time to time that are not good. I must ask her to forgive me. I have to tell her our son is in heaven with Jesus. I saw him! Perhaps she'll decide to turn to the Lord if I tell her what

I saw." He took Tara's hand. "Please understand my heart and how urgent this is. I have to do this. Do I have your blessing, Tara? Will you help me find her?"

"Yes, I understand, and I'll do all I can to help you find her." Tara put her arms around her husband. "You need to make peace with her, Scott, and ask her forgiveness. You must tell her about your dream. She needs Jesus. She will never have peace without Him."

Fran was now fifty-two years old. Several years before, she had left the group of women she had associated with because that turned out to be empty as well. She was a loner. She went to work and came home. She had no social life at all.

She was getting ready to move from her apartment to a place on the outskirts of town, and while cleaning out her drawers, she spotted the little wordless book. Her mind went back to the attempted suicide and the nurse who had given her that little book so many years ago. Her first thought was to just throw it in the pile with all the other trash, but she paused for a moment and looked at it. Tears ran down her face, and she fell across her bed and wept.

"Where were you when he died? How can you be a God of love?" She cried herself to sleep.

The next morning, as she was frantically rushing around trying to gather her projects together for work, the phone rang. She tripped over the large wicker laundry basket trying to get to the ringing phone. As she grabbed the phone, she knocked her coffee cup over, and coffee spilled on the papers she had written for work, and it soaked into the print. She cussed as she grabbed the handset of the phone.

"Hello," she gasped, breathless and annoyed.

"Fran? Is that you?" The voice was somewhat familiar.

"Yes. Who's this?"

"Fran, this is Scott."

She just stood there, stunned, about to hang up the phone.

"Please, Fran, don't hang up. I have to talk with you. Please! It's very important."

"We have nothing to talk about." Her hands shook and tears welled in her eyes.

"We have a lot to talk about, Fran, and the first thing I must say is I'm so sorry for all I did to hurt you. I am so sorry about our son." His voice shook with emotion. "It was all my fault. I take full responsibility for his death. I know you never wanted that for him. Please forgive me for all the pain I've caused you."

"Forgive you? I hope you're kidding! Forgive you for robbing me of the only child I would ever have? I've lived a life of hell, and you want me to forgive you? I hate you! I—" She started to cry. Shaking uncontrollably, she reached to hang up the phone.

"He's in heaven! I saw him," Scott shouted.

She caught his words as she was hanging up. She stopped and stood in the middle of the room, speechless. She drew the phone back to her ear.

"Fran, I'm a Christian now. I've received God's forgiveness for all my sins. I have given our son to the Lord. I was plagued with guilt for years over what I did to him and to you. He is a God of love and forgiveness, and He loves us. He forgave me, and He will forgive you and heal all of your brokenness."

She was silent as he continued.

Scott and Fran's little boy

"I had a dream, and I saw a little blonde curly-headed boy standing in front of me. I saw our son. He's safe, and he is surrounded by love. I want you to see him, too. Please, Fran, turn to Jesus, and ask him to save you. He will! You can be with Jesus and our child one day." Scott broke down and cried. "Please, Fran, I'm begging you!"

She looked toward her bedroom and saw the little book, still lying on the bed. Warm tears rolled down her face. "Where was your God when you pushed me into killing our son, Scott? Where has He been all these years while I've suffered and wanted to die? Tell me, Scott, where was your God the day I saw our child lying on a blue pad in that house of horror? Where?" She broke into sobs.

"He was right there, Fran. He was there. We were the ones—I was the one who made such a deadly choice."

"I don't want to talk about this anymore." She hung up the phone and fell to the floor sobbing. All the pain from so many years before swept over her like relentless waves. She was drowning in regret and hopelessness with no one to pull her to safety. "I can't live with this. I can't!" She called in sick and lay in bed for days.

Several days later, she dragged herself out of bed. She ran a brush through her hair, put on a little makeup and walked to the convenience store to buy coffee. It was Wednesday night, and she noticed people walking into the church near her apartment. She stopped and watched them.

A white-haired woman approached her. "Would you like to join us? We would love to have you."

"No, I don't go to church." She turned to walk away.

"It's very casual tonight. I think you would really enjoy it." The woman reached out and touched Fran's hand. "I'll sit in the back in case you decide to come." She flashed a genuine smile and turned to walk away, but she suddenly paused and turned around as she pulled something out of her black pocketbook. "I think I'm supposed to give this to you. This changed my life many years ago." She handed Fran a tattered little book. "A nurse gave this to me when I was in the hospital many years ago. She knew that this little book with no words would save my life."

Fran looked down and realized that she was holding the same little colorful wordless book that she had been given years before in that hospital room after her failed suicide. The same little book that she had found in her drawer just the night before. She stood there stunned. It couldn't be!

How could all of this be happening? First, Scott's call after all those years and his story about their little son in heaven. Now this. She sat down on a bench near the door of the church. With trembling hands, she started to go through the small colorful pages and read the explanation of each color on the back cover.

"The black page stands for sin. The Bible tells us, 'All have and sinned and fall short of the glory of God.'[14] Everyone is guilty of sin. We walk in darkness and can't find our way. There is fear, dread, and regret in the darkness of sin.

The red page stands for the blood of Jesus which was shed for our salvation. He died for our sins, He was buried, and He was raised three days later.[15]

The white page stands for the cleansing of salvation. Once we accept Christ, we become a new creation. He washes away all our sins and makes us white as snow. He forgives us![16]

The gold page stands for heaven. Jesus has gone to prepare a place for those who accept Him. We will live forever with Him in this beautiful place. [17]

The Green cover reminds us that we must grow in His love. We need to study His Word, and have fellowship with other believers."

Fran stared at the little book and wept.

After about fifteen minutes, she got up and walked inside the church. She saw the woman on the back pew and sat down next to her.

"I prayed you would come." The woman smiled as she patted Fran's hand.

The pastor said, "Turn in your Bibles to Psalm 40." He read,

'I waited patiently for the LORD; He turned to me and he heard my cry.

He lifted me out of the slimy pit, out of the mud and the mire;

He set my feet upon a rock and gave me a firm place to stand. He put a new song in my mouth, a hymn of praise to our God.

Many will see and fear the Lord and put their trust in Him. '

"It's God's will to lift us up and out of the slimy pit where we have allowed ourselves to dwell. He has a plan for our lives, and it's for good, and not for evil. He forgives us of all of our transgressions, and He will put a new song in our mouth. He will replace the pain with joy. The joy of the Lord is our strength. He understands our pain. He sees our mistakes, but He loves us, and He longs for us to set our feet on the rock Jesus. Are you in a pit tonight? Have you been suffocating in that pit for years? Then take His hand, and let Him set you free. He will pull you out tonight!"

A group came to the front and picked up their instruments and began to sing a medley of old hymns:

Aria

"At the cross, at the cross where I first saw the light,

And the burden of my heart rolled away,

It was there by faith I received my sight,

And now I am happy all the day!"

"Turn your eyes upon Jesus,

Look full in His wonderful face;

And the things of earth will grow strangely dim

In the light of His glory and grace."

"Amazing grace how sweet the sound that saved a wretch like me!

I once was lost, but now am found, was blind but now I see."

Fran couldn't contain the tears. She put her head in her hands and wept.

"If you want to make Jesus the Lord of your life tonight, come to Him. I will be here to pray with you." The pastor's words went straight to her heart.

She looked to the woman sitting next to her and took her hand.

"Do you want to go forward to pray?" Tears glistened in the woman's eyes.

"Yes, I do." Fran stood.

It seemed like a long walk to the front of that church, but with every step it was like heavy weights were falling off of her deeply burdened spirit. She reached the front and prayed with the pastor. She could hardly get the words out because she was crying from the depth of her being. She poured out years of grief and guilt to the Lord. Things buried inside for years rose to the surface.

They finally said, "amen."

The pastor said, "We have a new sister in Christ tonight. Her name is Fran."

The congregation broke out in applause.

"I'm free at last," she cried, as her new friend and the others joined her at the front of the church. "For so many years I have been sinking, and now He pulled me up. Thank you, Lord Jesus. Thank you. Thank you! You are my Rock. You are my Rock!"

"My name is Betty." The woman who had been sitting with her wiped away tears. "I am here for you, Fran." She hugged Fran for the longest time. She just didn't let go. It was as though the Lord was holding on to Fran through the arms of that dear woman.

"We're having a 'Healing of the Heart' seminar next Saturday, Fran." Betty smiled. "I think you would love being there. I believe it's your time. It's God's perfect timing."

"I'll be there." Fran took Betty's hands in hers. "I need everything I can get. I've been starving for years. I've been dead inside."

***

That Saturday about seventy women showed up. The speaker took the microphone and began to address the ladies.

"Today we are going to deal with the hurts that have kept you in bondage. Many of you have been held prisoners by the choices you have made in the past. It's time to be set free."

Many tears were shed that day as they discussed sexual abuse, physical abuse, rejection, addictions, divorce, the loss of a loved one, miscarriage, and abortion. When the word abortion was mentioned, Fran felt her hands begin to sweat. Her heart pounded in her chest.

"You must know that those tiny ones are received into the arms of Jesus. You will see them one day, but I believe it is good to name your child. It gives your baby personhood. Tonight I would like you to write a letter to your baby. Say what has been locked up in your heart for years, and then we are going to put those letters into this basket, and they will be left there. It is finished. I know that many of you do not know what the gender of your baby was, but pray, and let the Lord give you his or her name."

Weeping broke out in the room. Many women had lost children through miscarriage, and they were finally getting the closure they so desperately needed after such a painful loss. So many women who had abortions finally learned that they must confess to the sin of murder. They realized that day that there is no pretty way to cover up sin with euphemisms such as, "I terminated my pregnancy," or "It was just a fetus," or even the words, "I aborted the fetus."

To be free, we have to confess our sin, and He is faithful and just to forgive us of our sin and cleanse us of all unrighteousness. The women were reminded that Jesus loves us so much and He will forgive all sin, including the sin of murder.

Fran wept as she wrote the letter to her son. She asked the Lord, *"What do I name him?"*

Immediately she heard a still small voice say, *"His name is Jared."*

She smiled and wrote the name down and turned to the girl on her left. "I have a son waiting for me in heaven. His name is Jared."

They cried and hugged one another. She walked up to the front of the church and dropped her letter to Jared into the basket. She went back to her seat and worshipped the Lord.

The Holy Spirit was moving all over that room. He was setting women free from the deep bondage that had held them captive for years. What a glorious day it was! There was rejoicing in heaven. Those whom the Son sets free are free indeed!

As Fran grew in the Lord, she became involved in a crisis pregnancy center as a counselor to pregnant women. She talked with the women with great compassion, and she pleaded with them to choose life for their babies. She stayed late in the evening to talk with the girls who were determined to choose death for their children.

One night, after Fran had talked with a client for two hours, the woman got up and said, "I've heard enough. I'm having the abortion. I'm not ready to be a mother." She bolted for the door.

Fran followed her. "You're already a mother. You became a mother the moment you conceived your son or daughter. The question isn't whether you are a mother. The question is, will you deliver a living baby or a dead baby? Please. I beg you. Don't do what I did. I killed my son! I was in my second trimester, and I saw his little body lying on a table in that abortion chamber. They mutilated him. He was the only child I would ever have. I have suffered for years, and only recently have I experienced healing and forgiveness from the Lord. Don't do what I did. I beg you!"

That woman stopped at the door. "You saw him?" She turned around.

"Yes, I saw him. I saw my dead baby. I beg you, please don't do this. It will destroy you." Tears streamed down Fran's face.

The woman went back to the overstuffed chair and fell into it. "What can you do to help me?" She began to cry. "I need help. Please help me."

Fran's story saved the lives of many children. She spoke at many events, sharing about her son, Jared. She touched the lives of so many. One night, after a meeting where she was the guest speaker, a man in his late fifties walked up to her.

His eyes were filled with tears as he held his wife's hand. "Hello, Fran. I'm so proud of you."

She looked intently into his eyes. "Scott?" Her mouth dropped open.

"He smiled as he took her hand. "Yes, Fran. It's been many years. This is my wife, Tara. Thank you for naming our son. Jared is a wonderful name. My son has a name!" Tears ran down his face as he squeezed Tara's hand. "I will look for Jared when I get to heaven, Fran. I'm so happy for you. I'm so happy you met Jesus. You are a powerful voice for Him."

Tears welled up and spilled over onto Fran's face. "Hello, Tara. It's a pleasure to meet you." She reached out and hugged Tara, and then her eyes turned to Scott. "Jared will be waiting for you, Scott. You won't have to look for him." She reached out and hugged Scott, and the tears flowed, but they were good tears. Tears of forgiveness and restoration.

If any chains remained that bound up the two of them, they fell off that night. God is so full of mercy and grace. Oh, the joy and the power of forgiveness! It unlocks the cold and broken heart, and it releases the heart song to sing once again.

That night the angels rejoiced. They shouted praises as these two people who had been broken and filled with regret and pain for so many years finally made peace with one another. Yes, they had made peace with God long before that night, but forgiveness is freedom. It is the essential ingredient for our soul to be set free from chains that bind up our hearts and strangle our spirit. Such release. Such joy!

Chapter Nine—See You at the Gate

Describing heaven is like trying to communicate with someone without knowing their language. We see through a mirror darkly, but one day we will see Him face to face. We know bits and pieces, but one day we will understand completely, even as He knows us completely. Time, sorrow, doubt, fear, and disappointments do not exist in that beautiful place called heaven.

Cindy's son, Christian, wanted so much to see his mother come to the great city, but when the Great Shepherd told him that his mother had chosen not to come, he realized that it was a sad and tragic choice that multitudes make. He had longed to meet her, but there was no turning back time, and there is no mourning in heaven. Eternity holds so many priceless promises, and there is much to do. The residents forever praise and worship the Son of God and the Father of Lights. They wait for the day when a fallen world will be redeemed by Jesus. No more sin, no more hate, and no more death!

Angels gather around the great white throne of the Father of Lights praising and worshiping continually. Their praises are heard all over the kingdom. It's a constant melody of love and glory such as no ear on earth has ever heard, or anyone has even dreamed of. Memories of all the struggles and pain on earth vaporize in such glory.

Oh, yes, with great anticipation the angels and the residents of heaven wait for Jesus to return to earth. That will be a most blessed day for many, and a most horrible day for all who have rejected Him. It will be horror beyond imagination to see the King whom they had rejected. Prayer changes hearts, and how crucial it is to intercede for those who do not know His love and grace.

***

Brandon approached the angels as they broke out in exuberant praise. "Another soul has given her heart to the King," one of the angels shouted. "It's your Melody, Brandon. It's your daughter!" The angel embraced Brandon. "Melody has come to the Master. She will be coming home to reside with us forever. She and her mother will be with us for eternity."

Joyful shouts came from Brandon's lips as Aria, Joel, and multitudes of others rejoiced in such a great salvation. Heaven is a great celebration of love! It never ends because redeemed souls continue to flood the gates.

"It won't be long now, and they will be leaving there. It won't be long, and they'll be coming home." Brandon's face beamed with heavenly joy.

***

Susan lived a comfortable and fulfilling life, but shadows of the three children she never held haunted her. Two of the deaths were out of her control, but Aria died because of her choice.

Were the other two children victims of that choice as well? Did the abortion weaken her body and cause her to miscarry the others? That question haunted her. It gnawed deep inside her. It hid so deep she failed to realize it was there.

Jeff had always been concerned about her waves of depression, and her mood swings, but Susan had a very difficult time expressing the pain and guilt buried so deep inside. She brushed off his questions and concerns.

Their daughter, Jewel, grew up and fell in love with Jason, a young man who loved Jesus. Jason's beliefs were foreign but intriguing to her. He shared with her the beautiful story of God's love, and how God the Father had sent

Jesus the Son into the world to pay such a terrible price for the sins of mankind.

Jewel was full of questions. Jason patiently shared the Scriptures with her and lovingly explained how she could apply them to her life. One night they were in a deep discussion, and Jason gently took Jewel's hand.

"He's been chasing after you all of your life, Jewel. His love is never-ending, and He longs for you to love Him in return. Don't you think it's time to quit running from the one who laid down His life for you, and turn around and embrace His love?"

Jewel began to cry. "I've never heard of such love. It's amazing! He has given you to me, Jason. You are the love of my life. What a gift you are. I want to receive Jesus into my life. I want to serve Him at your side forever."

As they prayed together that June night, there was great joy and celebration in heaven. Oh, if only they could have seen the rejoicing that was going on because another precious lamb had come home to the Shepherd. They would see it one day. Oh yes, they would see it throughout eternity!

They planned their wedding to give honor to the covenant they had made to Jesus the King and to one another.

Susan and Jeff were more than overwhelmed by the great change in their daughter. They were excited about the upcoming wedding, and they spent many hours with Jewel and Jason discussing the details.

"This will be a covenant between us and the Lord," Jason said, as they visited with the folks one evening. "We want our marriage to honor Him, and we want everyone present to feel His presence. This will be a great celebration of our love for one another and a celebration of our covenant of love for Him."

All of this talk about God puzzled Susan and Jeff. They saw an obvious change in their daughter. She had a peace about her, a peace like they had never seen. Rather than being stressed and nervous like she had been for years, she seemed to be filled with joy.

One night after dinner, Jewel sat with her parents in the family room, and she began to share her heart with them. "Mom and Dad, you have accomplished so much in your lives. You are successful and comfortable, and you have been wonderful parents, but there is a piece missing in your lives, a void that only God can fill."

She moved next to her mom and put her arm around her neck. "Mom, I know that deep inside there is a hurt, a wound that has been festering for years, and none of us can reach down and heal it. God knows what it is, and only His love can pluck it out of you. Only He can heal you."

Susan began to cry. Jeff put his arm around her as he fought back the tears. His voice trembled. "I've always felt that we are the god of our own destiny, Jewel. I never have believed in a creator, or a Savior, but I see something in you that I have never seen before."

Susan broke down and sobbed and put her head on Jeff's shoulder.

"You see Jesus in me, Mom. You see Jesus in me! He wants to be a part of your lives. People will see Him in you, as well. He asks us to repent of our sins and turn to Him, and we can become a new creation. He is calling you and Dad. We can spend eternity together with all of those we love. Many are in heaven waiting for you."

"Do you believe that children go to heaven, Jewel? Even those who were never born?"

Susan's hands trembled as Jewel took them both in hers.

"Mom, the scripture says in Jeremiah, "Before I formed you in the womb, I knew you." She opened her Bible to Psalm 139:13–16 and handed it to Jeff. "Please read this, Dad."

He read, *"For you created my inmost being; you knit me together in my mother's womb."* Tears spilled down his cheeks. *"I praise you because I am fearfully and wonderfully made; your works are wonderful, I know that full well. My frame was not hidden from you when I was made in the secret place, when I was woven together in the depths of the earth. Your eyes saw my unformed body; all the days ordained for me were written in your book before one of them came to be."*

Jeff broke down. "Susan, I believe this is answering our questions about the two children we lost."

The three of them embraced and wept together.

"I know how much you have hurt all these years over the two children you lost, Mom." Jewel's words reached deep into her mother's agonizing memories.

"Three babies. There were three babies."
Susan broke into sobs. She sat there awhile in
silence. She tried to catch her breath before she
continued. "I aborted a child when I was in
college. I'm so sorry. Oh, God. I am so sorry!"

A look of pain and shock shot across
Jeff's face, and suddenly it all made sense. The
periods of depression, the unexplained anger,
the distancing herself even from him, and even
the way she felt so driven by her work.

Jewel embraced her mother. "He will
forgive you, and He will set your heart free.
Will you ask him to forgive you of your sins?
Will you finally give your little babies to Him?
He's had them in His care all these years, Mom.
Will you accept Him as your Lord and Savior?

He has been waiting for you. They have been waiting for you, Mom."

"I will." Jeff took Jewel's hand as he fought tears. "I know I've tried to do this by myself all my life. Today I give my life to Him. I give it up. I surrender!"

Susan looked over at her daughter and her husband as they embraced. Her tears were like a well that had sprung up from deep within, spilling out years of guilt, pain, and regret. "I will give my life to Him, Jewel. I will."

They sat together on the sofa and prayed. Celebration broke out in heaven as the King and all the residents of heaven rejoiced in the knowledge that two more lost souls had heard

the Shepherd's song and had come home at last.
What victory. What joy!

**

Brandon scooped Aria up in his arms. "Susan has entered the sheep gate. She was lost, but now she is found. Susan, your mother, and Jeff, her husband, have come to know the great love that was shed abroad for the souls of many. They have accepted His sacrifice, and they are free. We must tell the others!"

Aria skipped with joy through the garden holding onto Brandon's hand. They ran to tell Joel, and on the way, they spotted Aria's brother and sister playing with the animals. There are no stepchildren in heaven. We are all part of God's family. That is a wonderful thing!

"Eden. Jacob. It's mother. She has come to Jesus. She will be coming to us soon. She's coming home. Jeff, your father, is coming as well!"

All the angels and all the children around them began praising God, the Father of Lights. They sang and danced with joy. As they sang, their glorious melody mingled with resounding praise and worship throughout the kingdom. It all blended together in perfect harmony. The Great Shepherd laughed as they danced and sang. Their voices radiated love as they sang:

"Come home, come home,

you who are weary, come home;

earnestly, tenderly, Jesus is calling,

calling, O sinner, come home!"

"Just as I am, without one plea,

But that Thy blood was shed for me,

And that Thou bidd'st me come to Thee,

Oh Lamb of God, I come! I come!

***

It seemed like a blink of an eye in heaven, but it was twenty years later that a beautiful young woman entered through the East gate. She was in her seventies on earth, but everyone is in their prime in heaven. She was escorted through the gates by Daniel, a tall, stately angel. As she entered the great city, many were calling her name.

"Fran! Fran! Welcome home!"

She was greeted with laughter and sweet embraces. Fran was awestruck at the beauty all around her. It was more than she could take in. Her eyes searched through the throng of welcomers. Suddenly she spotted a young boy making his way through the cheering multitude. He held a bouquet of beautiful yellow roses. She ran towards the blonde, blue-eyed boy, and cried, "Jared. Jared! My son. Jared. My son!"

He ran to her and wrapped his arms around her neck and held her tight. As He handed her the lovely bouquet of flowers, cheers filled the kingdom.

"I knew you were coming, Mommy. We've all been waiting for you. We welcome you home." He threw his arms around her neck again, and they held each other ever so tightly.

The King approached, and Fran fell at his feet. All of the pain she had suffered on earth was gone in a breath, never to be remembered. The King pulled her gently to her feet and looked deeply into her eyes. "Well done, my good and faithful servant. You have been faithful with a few things; I will put you in charge of many things. For as much as you've done it to the least of my brethren, you've done it unto me. Enter in to your rest."

All heaven rejoiced!

It was a blessed day when Scott came through the gate. Fran was right when she told him that he wouldn't have to look for their son. As he entered, Jared stood waiting. Scott burst into praise. Standing directly in front of him was the child that he had turned over to death so many years before. He knew that face. He had seen it in a dream.

"Daddy!" Jared cried, as he ran to hug him. "Daddy. We are so happy that you are a part of God's great kingdom. Now we will be together for eternity!"

Scott lifted him up in his arms. "My Jared. How beautiful you are! Oh, how absolutely beautiful you are. How I have longed for this day." Scott walked through the crowd shouting, "Look. This is my son, Jared. This is my son!"

Scott and Jared

What a miraculous event! Only God's love could bring something so amazing to pass. Like Scott, we make many poor choices in this life. We hurt so many people with careless decisions and cruel words, but the blood of Jesus cleanses us from all that sin, and it's as though it never happened. This is true joy. The joy of the Lord is our strength![18]

Aria

***

The tiny broken ones continued to come through the gates from all over the world. It caused great pain for the Master and all of heaven to see the millions of thrown-away children. There seemed to be no end to the senseless bloodshed. Reports were breaking out on the news in America, a once Christian nation, that abortion profiteers were actually selling the parts of the broken babies … such an abomination.!

Oh, how planet earth had fallen. It made the angels weep.

Angels Weep

Sin had taken over the hearts and minds of millions. The world became darker and darker, and sin abounded more and more. The hearts of many had become cold, and they loved the created things rather than the creator. They uttered blasphemies, and their sins knew no limit. They exchanged the truth of God for a lie.

The Word of God, as it is written in 2 Chronicles 7:14, cried out to the people of America and the rest of the world, but who would listen and be saved? *"If my people, who are called by my name, will humble themselves and pray and seek my face and turn from their wicked ways, then I will hear from heaven, and I will forgive their sin and will heal their land."*

Millions of followers of the King were brutally murdered simply because they loved Him. There was a strong diabolical hatred for the Shepherd and His people. Demon-possessed terrorists drove Christians from their homes. They crucified them and beheaded them. Oh, woe to the earth!

Their judgment was indeed drawing near. Time was running out for the planet earth. Mankind had destroyed it. They had no respect for life from the tiniest of humanity to the aged.

An avalanche of sin blinded them to truth and buried their consciences. They turned themselves over to a reprobate mind, and they practiced sins that were an abomination to the Father of Lights. They refused to turn back. Woe, woe to earth and its inhabitants!

The King knew there was little time for the people of earth to get their lives in order, but they had to make a decision to choose life or death.

He had spoken to them through His Word long ago, as it is written in Deuteronomy 30:19, *"I call the heavens and the earth as witnesses against you that I set before you life and death, blessings and curses. Now choose life, so that you and your children may live."*

They hadn't made the right choice. They chose death. Their laws were corrupt and promoted the killing of their unborn children. The ground was stained by innocent blood. They mocked His name, but much to their sorrow their mocking would quickly cease when Jesus split the sky and broke through the clouds with a host of His saints with Him!

It was like the days of Noah, but this time the Lord Jesus would be the ark of safety. The door was open for any who would to come in. Those in heaven knew that they would ride with the King very soon. There was a sense of preparation in heaven and a great anticipation on earth. It seemed as though the earth itself groaned and travailed as it awaited His return, but the people refused to repent of their wicked ways.

It is God's will that all would come to repentance. It is not His will that even one would perish, but millions choose the way of death. If only they could see through that veil. If only they knew what they would be missing throughout eternity. If only they knew the torment that awaits those who choose darkness. It makes one tremble.

***

The day Susan walked through the gate, Aria, Brandon, Joel, Eden and Jacob, and hundreds of others who had known her throughout her life on earth were waiting. She was a sight to see as she entered the kingdom through the East Gate escorted by that majestic angel.

Jesus stood at the gate as she entered. She looked radiant as her dark auburn hair fell against her velvet complexion. Her brown eyes sparkled with life. The deep facial lines, the gray hair, and the weak heart that had all been a part of her later days on earth were shed the moment she left her earthly body behind. That body was like an empty tent lying in the hospital bed. She needed it no longer. It was a warm evening in June when her spirit took flight in the arms of the angel. A new and vibrant life now stood before the King and all the people who had known her.

"Oh. the beauty! The beauty," she cried.

Her eyes were wide with wonder as she looked at the crystal clear River of Life that flowed from the throne of God and of the Lamb down the middle of the golden street of the city. On each side of the river stood the Tree of Life. She remembered reading about that tree when she studied Revelation with her family.

"Blessed are those who wash their robes, that they may have the right to the Tree of Life and may go through the gates into the city," she whispered. "There it is. I am here. There it is. He washed me in His precious blood!"

"Welcome home, Susan." The King reached out His nail-scarred hands to her.

She immediately recognized her Lord and Savior. She knelt at his feet and worshipped

Him. What a sight it was. Applause and praise erupted in the great city.

She was overcome by the many familiar faces standing there to greet her. She was surrounded by those she had loved. Her grandparents, whom she had loved and depended on so much in her younger years, embraced her. Cousins and many friends and co-workers rushed to greet her. There, in the midst of them, stood her mother who had died when Susan was ten years old, and her father who had died when she was eighteen. She recognized them immediately. They were strikingly beautiful and youthful.

Aria, Eden, and Jacob walked together to greet her. The sight of them was breathtaking!

Brandon and Joel stood back and grasped hands.

"Welcome, Mother. We welcome you home. We've been waiting for you. I am Aria, your first child, and this is Jacob, your son, and Eden, your daughter."

Cheering could be heard all over the kingdom. The voices of the angels, the saints, and the children growing in the garden all blended beautifully into an opera of praise and celebration. You could hear the brush of the wings, and the sounds of the cherubim and seraphim who worshipped the heavenly Father continually with extravagant praise around that glorious throne. Oh, such joy!

Susan stared at them with wonderment, and she looked back at Jesus as He smiled and nodded.

"Aria. What a beautiful name." Susan was in awe. "I knew you would be here. Jewel said you would be here. You are a work of art. Jacob and Eden. My babies. My babies. How absolutely beautiful you are. All three of you are here with me at last. All three of you."

She ran to her children and swept them into her arms. She held them and kissed them, and she knew at that moment that they would never be separated again. She was home!

The world was now behind her, and instantly it became a fleeting memory. Years of great struggle, regret, pain, and suffering were gone forever. She knew that this was home.

This is what God intended for all of his

children, but like her, they had to answer the

invitation to come. They had to open the door to

Him before they could enter the gates of His

kingdom.

Aria looked up at her mother with such

love, and then she let go of Susan's hand as she

looked at Jesus. Aria walked up to him and took

His hand.

"Thank you." she said, looking into those

beautiful, loving eyes. "Thank you for paying

such a price for all of us. Thank you for

preparing such a magnificent place for us."

She looked at the wounds in his hands and ran her fingers over them, and then she looked down at his wounded feet.

"Oh, how He loves us. The Lamb of God is the King of Kings, and Lord of Lords. All the world will bow to you on that great and terrible day. Thank you for loving us," she said over and over. She knelt at His feet and worshipped her Redeemer. And all of heaven rejoiced. He is worthy of all praise!

Aria walked back to her mother and embraced her. Love radiated and flowed. It wound its beauty around each and every saint of God standing there. It flooded the garden with its warmth, it flowed down the great river, and it rose to the highest peaks of heaven's mountains. It rushed into the streams and waters, and it blew like a gentle wind through the trees as it sang its magnificent song. The angels spread their giant wings and shouted,

"For God so loved the world that He gave his only son, and whosoever believes in Him shall never perish, but have everlasting life!"[19]

A thunderous cheer rang throughout the entire Kingdom. Michael stood at attention next to Aria and Susan. He spread his massive wings and shouted,

"Holy! Holy! Holy! is the Lord God Almighty! Who was, and is, and is to come!" Then he folded his beautiful, massive wings around the two of them, and a single tear fell from his ebony eyes—a tear of joy and victory.

And they continue to come through the beautiful gates; millions of them. They live forever in the presence of the great King. They are all waiting ... waiting to see you at the gate!

THE BEGINNING

"Welcome Home"

He will wipe every tear from their eyes.

There will be no more death or mourning or

crying or pain, for the old order of things has

passed away—Revelation 21:4

However, as it is written: "What no eye

has seen, what no ear has heard, and what no

human mind has conceived"—the things God

has prepared for those who love him—

1 Corinthians 2:9

Conclusion—It's Your Time Now

Do you see yourself in one or more of the characters in this book? Are you pregnant and frightened? Do you feel there is no way out? There is a way, and His name is Jesus. He is there right now to help you and to set you free from all guilt and sin. He will direct you to people who will love you and help you and your child. If you are pregnant and alone, there are pregnancy help centers that will stand by you and walk through this journey with you. You and your baby have a future and a hope. Your life, and the life of your little child, are a treasure to God.

Have you had an abortion, or perhaps more than one? Do you identify with Susan, Fran, or Cindy? Have you bottled up the guilt and shame? Do you pretend that nothing is eating away at you? Are you carrying with you the ghost of a little child who haunts your life day after day? This was never God's will for your life. You, like those you just read about, can be free of all guilt and shame. All you have to do is ask Him into your heart. Ask Him to forgive you, and He will. Tell Him about the things you have buried deep inside for so long, and let Him cleanse you from the top of your head to the soles of your feet. He died for you. He loves you, and He longs to have fellowship with you. He invites you into His kingdom to rejoice in His love forever.

Maybe you are the father of an aborted child and, like Scott, you thought you were doing the right thing when you choose abortion. Deep inside you feel the loss and the guilt like millions of other dads. You may have been a teenager at the time of the decision, or perhaps you were in college and felt that the timing was off. Whatever the reason, you made a choice to end your child's life—a tragic and heartbreaking choice. You can find help and forgiveness. You may be able to make amends with the baby's mother as Scott did, or maybe that is not possible. You don't have to carry the weight of this little child around with you for the rest of your life. It's time to put it all at the feet of Jesus.

Many have lost children in death. I lost two babies through miscarriage, and the grief was so personal and so deep. It was hard to hear comments from well-meaning friends like, "Oh, you can always have another one," or, "At least it happened early in your pregnancy."

We must walk through our pain, and many times those closest to us don't understand, but we love them anyway. There is no room for bitterness. Don't blame God, and don't blame yourself. I know that after my miscarriages I felt that maybe it was my fault. Maybe if I had rested more, or maybe I was too active, maybe, maybe, maybe …

Losing a loved one can make us angry and bitter toward God. We can choose to run to Him, or we can choose to run from Him. As we have learned from Cindy's story, bitterness will eat you alive. Allow God to wrap His arms around you and bring you comfort.

I was at a healing seminar years ago helping other women deal with their loss. The Lord began to deal with me, and I began weeping uncontrollably. I was so busy helping others that I didn't realize my own scars were still buried deep inside.

I felt the presence of the Holy Spirit come over me and He said, *What about your children? What are their names?*

I sat there for several minutes as tears fell from my eyes.

I heard myself say, "Their names are Bethany and Josiah."

I was set free that day, along with so many that I was ministering to. I long for the day when those children meet me at the gate. What a day that will be!

Dear friends of mine lost their son at the age of thirty-three in a car accident. It devastated their lives. Another dear mom lost her son, Brandon, to cancer at the age of thirty-two. Brandon's widow, Christina, is a strong Christian girl, but every day she faces the challenges of raising her precious little girl, Aria, without her father. Aria was only about six weeks old when Brandon went home to Jesus. They have been an inspiration to me in the writing of this book. They love Jesus, and, yes, the end of their story will be a good one. Both of these families cling to God's promises for daily strength. They couldn't wake up each day without His presence. He is their Rock and their salvation.

Have you ever asked Jesus into your heart? You can be religious, but not saved by His grace. Going to church doesn't save anyone. If you have any doubt about your salvation, you can pray a prayer like this:

Dear Lord, I'm a sinner. I'm in such need. Please forgive me for all my sins, and please cleanse me. I invite you into my life. Take up residence in me. Be the Lord of my life that I might serve you forever. Heal my broken heart today. I receive you now as my Lord and my Savior. Thank you for dying in my place and paying the price for my sins. I look forward to spending eternity with you and those I love. In Jesus' name. Amen.

You are here for a reason, and He has a purpose for your life. If you are just entering His kingdom, find a good Bible-believing church that will help you grow in His love. You need others to encourage you and to mentor you. Get a modern translation of the Bible such as the New Living Bible, and read it every time you have a chance. It's God's love letter to you. As Steve told Joel, "It is food for your soul."

If you need prayer, we are here for you. We treasure you. God bless you on your journey. Grow in His love, and reach out to others. He will use you to further His kingdom. Go light the world!

About The Author

Penny Lea

On June 7, 1982, Penny Lea had a supernatural experience in a little church cemetery just outside Nashville, Tennessee. She suddenly heard the cries of what seemed to be thousands of children. The cries became louder and louder, and she was so overwhelmed that she ran from that place. The Lord spoke to her:

Don't run from this. I am putting a new anointing on your life, your music, and your ministry.

"Who are these children, and where are they?" Her cries went up to the Lord daily.

Weeks later, and after much prayer, the Lord revealed to her who the children were. They were aborted babies ... they were the broken ones. She knew that God was calling her to be His voice for those who had no voice. She couldn't run from this.

Penny has spoken before thousands. She shared the platform with Mother Teresa in Ottawa, Canada, before 32,000 people as they stood in the rain. She was a guest at the Reagan White House and has led thousands in pro-life marches throughout America. She has been the founder of pregnancy centers in Minnesota and Florida, where hundreds of babies have been saved. She has encouraged and assisted many in starting pregnancy help centers around the United States and Canada.

Penny Lea is the author of "Sing A Little Louder," the most-read pro-life story in America. The story has spread throughout the world and has been translated into many languages. Recently, a short film by that same name has been released. It will be shown throughout America and the world. Penny Lea is presently traveling and bringing her message along with the film to all who will listen. This story is gripping.

"It's a cry to the sleeping Church. It's a cry to come out of our apathy and stand in the gap for the oppressed," Penny says. "I pray this film will help us awaken a sleeping giant, the Church , to a holocaust that has claimed nearly sixty million children and has destroyed countless millions who have been held captive by its deadly grasp. It is also a cry for the persecuted Church in the Middle East who is being brutally murdered by ISIS as most of the world stands silent. We must intervene. One day we'll hear the haunting words from our Savior, '*Where were you when they were killing my babies and my persecuted people?' Let the Church be the Church!*"

Penny Lea is the mother of six children here on earth and two children in heaven. She and her husband, Harry, adopted one of their sons when he was fifteen years old. They are strong advocates of adoption.

"My prayer for my children is that they would follow Jesus as long as they live and never compromise His principles. They are living in a different America and a different church age than I grew up in. Very little is said about sin anymore. The Church is more of a social club than a place of righteousness and restoration for the soul. It will take much perseverance to follow the Lord in these difficult times.

"My prayer for America is that this nation would repent and turn back to God. I believe the stench of our sins is nauseating to the nostrils of a righteous God. I live for the day when we see an end to the slaughter of our precious children."

The late David Wilkerson had this to say about her:

"Penny Lea literally shook Times Square Church. Hundreds of people were awakened to the crime of abortion. I have never heard so many confessions by women who were hiding this terrible secret. One girl confessed that she'd had twelve abortions. I believe that Penny Lea is called by God to help awaken America and shake up politicians regarding the spirit of murder now controlling the abortionists."

Penny says, "I wrote *Aria* as the Lord led me. The story just happened as I wrote. I have never written fiction, but then again, I have to ask myself, is this really fiction? I think not. I believe it is a glimpse into His marvelous kingdom. I pray it will be a message that will bring help and healing to those who are hurting. Abortion kills one life and destroys those left in its wake. I thank God for His mercy and His wonderful grace!"

Contact us at:

Penny Lea Ministries

PO Box 3226

Boone, NC 28607

Visit our website at www.pennylea.org

Visit our Facebook pages:

Penny lea Ministries

Sing A Little Louder

Penny Lea's blog

Aria

E-mail Penny at

pennylea60@yahoo.com

Endnotes

1 1John 1.9

2 John 3:17

3 Isaiah 53:5

4 John 8:36

5 Acts 16:31

6 Hebrews 3:7

7 Revelation 5:5

8 Matthew 24:27

9 Luke 23:30

10 Jeremiah 1:5

11 1 Corinthians 2:9

12 Romans 8:38-39

13 2 Corinthians 5:17

14 Romans 3:23

15 1 Corinthians 15:3-4

16 Isaiah 1:18

17 John 14:3

18 Nehemiah 8:10

19 John.3:16

Made in the USA
Columbia, SC
11 July 2022